Rich Girl Problems Series

Erotica: Books 1 - 4

Rita Rojas

Copyright © 2014 by Speedy Publishing LLC

All rights reserved. No part of this publication may be reproduced, distributed or transmitted in any form or by any means, including photocopying, recording, or other electronic or mechanical methods, without the prior written permission of the publisher, except in the case of brief quotations embodied in critical reviews and certain other noncommercial uses permitted by copyright law. For permission requests, write to the publisher, addressed "Attention: Permissions Coordinator," at the address below.

Speedy Publishing LLC (c) 2014
40 E. Main St., #1156
Newark, DE 19711
www.speedypublishing.co

Ordering Information:

Quantity sales; Special discounts are available on quantity purchases by corporations, associations, and others. For details, contact the "Special Sales Department" at the address above.

-- 1st edition

Manufactured in the United States of America

Warning

This book contains sexually explicit scenes and adult language. It may be considered offensive to some readers. This book is for sale to adults ONLY.

* * * * * * * * * * * * * * * * * *

Please store your books wisely where underage readers cannot access them

Table of Contents

Publisher's Notes i

Book 1: Worked Over 1

Book 2: Spanked Behind the Library 24

Book 3: Total Role-Play 44

Book 4: Job Opportunity 65

Publisher's Notes

Disclaimer

This publication is intended to provide helpful and informative material. It is not intended to diagnose, treat, cure, or prevent any health problem or condition, nor is intended to replace the advice of a physician. No action should be taken solely on the contents of this book. Always consult your physician or qualified health-care professional on any matters regarding your health and before adopting any suggestions in this book or drawing inferences from it.

The author and publisher specifically disclaim all responsibility for any liability, loss or risk, personal or otherwise, which is incurred as a consequence, directly or indirectly, from the use or application of any contents of this book.

Any and all product names referenced within this book are the trademarks of their respective owners. None of these owners have sponsored, authorized, endorsed, or approved this book.

Always read all information provided by the manufacturers' product labels before using their products. The author and publisher are not responsible for claims made by manufacturers.

Print Edition 2014

Book 1: Worked Over

The mediocre music in the club was blaring, reducing conversations to gestures and pantomimes. There were dozens of strobe, flood and multicolored spotlights that swiveled in an arc, while opening and closing its shutters briefly illuminating the faces and torsos of wallflowers and dance floor pros alike and making the room seem like a strange stop motion movie with human actors. Even without the strobe lights or eardrum weakening bass, the club was still filled with actors. There were teens too young to be there, gawking and excitedly talking to one another while trying not to stare but doing an adorably bad job of it. There were dancers who knew each song and followed the beats with their bodies, sometimes in pairs and sometimes alone, seeming in many ways as much a part of the atmosphere as the floodlights. There were the awkward and the not yet drunk, the much too drunk and a few try hard fellows, moving in a close formation and feeding off of one another to keep up the illusion of confidence and poise. Among all of these and many more people sat Stacy Chilton, watching the night play out from a small table 20 feet from the dance floor. She was exasperated, irritable and bored all at once, a combination of emotions that made her fall back into the reckless behavior she had always returned to ever since childhood, though at 22, some would argue that her childhood hadn't yet ended. Huffing slightly, she stood up, stretched and then began wandering around the club, hoping for something interesting to happen. As she moved past the dance floor a man asked her to dance and she obliged, trying to get lost in the music and motion but being unable to due to the motion of the man's hands roaming too far south far too quickly. Stacy rolled her eyes and let the song finish, shaking her head and trotting off when the man then tried to pull her closer to the center of the dance floor in what he thought was a subtle fashion. "Tease," he said as she moved further away from both him and the dance floor, reflecting on his observation as she did.

Soon enough she was at the bar among the far too drunk, just a bit drunk and soon to be drunk individuals. She sat on an empty stool between two men, one with his head down and his arm over his face and another in the same position who was surrounded by empty shot glasses. Horace the barman (and often her impromptu wingman) walked over to her and smiled bemusedly. "Stacy, you look great as always. What can I get you and how has your night been?" She shrugged "Do you have any liquid excitement Horace? My night has been hideously boring." Horace laughed and made a show of checking through all the cabinets before shrugging himself. "Sorry, fresh out of liquid excitement, how about a grasshopper instead?" Stacy nodded and watched Horace make the drink; his movement's quick and efficient, wasting no time with unneeded theatrics. Soon he sat the highball glass in front of her and smiled. "I just beat my personal record for that drink, aren't you happy for me?" She nodded with a grin before sipping the drink, feeling a bit less irritable once her glass was half full. She closed her eyes and enjoyed the taste and the sensation of the alcohol doing its work but was pulled abruptly from her enjoyment by a try hard fellow sitting down next to her in an extroverted, overly familiar manner while swiveling to look at her on his stool. He seemed to be almost orange from time at a tanning salon and had his hair spiked and a loud pink polo shirt on with a turned up collar, exactly like the friends of his that hovered around near him. "Hey there beautiful, buy you a drink?" He said with a smirk. Stacy gestured toward her half-finished grasshopper and shook her head. "No thanks, I've already got one." The fellows smirk remained were it had been. "Fair enough. Since I can't buy you a drink, can I have a bit of your time?" Stacy shrugged as disinterestedly as she could and sipped her drink once more before deciding to try having a simple conversation. "Sure, how's it going?" She said, causing the man's smirk to widen a bit as he leaned slightly closer to her and ordered a bull blaster. "It's going a lot better now, that's for sure. Wanna dance?" Stacy shook her head again "No, the music in there isn't my bag, it's the same old thing over and over, I'm looking for something different, you know?" The try hard thumped the empty cup down and nodded "I totally feel you, something different is where it's at, I'm all about being different too, great minds eh? My bros and I are the most different folks you'll ever meet, I've got the most stupidly tricked out ride in town, hands down, and I'm always trying to do different stuff, we should hang out somewhere different sometime, can I get your number?" "Sure, it's 232-9715" Stacy said with a grin while extending her hand. The fellow made a fist and lightly pressed it against her hand before making an exaggerated explosion noise and laughing along with his friends. "That's how my bros and I do it, how's THAT for different eh? We're about to go do donuts in the parking lot so we've gotta split, but I'll call you sometime, we can plan a totally different night out!" Stacy nodded enthusiastically and soon let her forced smile fade as the last of the group made his way out of the door to the club. Horace came back over and shook his head sadly. "That wasn't very nice, scrambling your phone number like that, good thing he didn't try it. I can't even blame you that time...what was that handshake thing?" Stacy laughed and imitated the noise and gesture. "I can't say it was charming, but in its own way it was sort of different I suppose." Horace shook his head again "Nah, it's from Placid Valley 10-1-3-2-1, they all do it at the end of each season finale...um, or so my daughters have told me." He said with chagrin. "Okay fine! I watched it a few times, so sue me!" Stacy laughed genuinely as Horace sat a fresh grasshopper in front of her. "You're horrid, laughing at an old man like that. Here's another grasshopper, never speak of this again." Stacy finished her drink and saw a tall, handsome man smiling at her from across the bar. After looking around and seeing no one else, Stacy returned his smile and then the man surprised her by calling Horace over to him and speaking to him for a bit. Horace chuckled and then came back over to Stacy and took her grasshopper, moving it near the man at the far end of the bar who was now smiling widely. Stacy was open mouthed at his audacity, wondering whether to be impressed or angry when Horace smiled at her and curled his finger at her. She sighed and walked over to the other end of the bar; sitting next to the man and taking her drink back with a huff. "I've had people buy me drinks from across the bar, but never steal mine." She said coolly while glaring at Horace. "Hey, you said you wanted something different and this guy's fitting the bill so far eh? I'm off, I've got barflies to swat and drunks to serve up!" The man extended his hand and Stacy shook it warily. "I'm James and in my defense, I relocated your drink to help you out, miss...?"

"I'm Stacy, pleased to meet you James. I'd be interested to know how relocating my drink was supposed to help me?" She said with a grin, enjoying the conversation already. "Well, instead of sitting between two drunks and looking like you're about to fall asleep, you're sitting next to me and at the least smiling." Stacy laughed and nodded, unable to deny the facts as they were. "I looked that bored?" She asked, getting a nod from James. "I don't even know why I come here anymore honestly, they play the same 9 songs, the dance floor is filled with phantom gropers and the bar is a shooting gallery for pick up artists. Horace is fun, but the routine here is just mind numbing." James looked thoughtful for a moment before responding. "Maybe it's not the routine here that bores you, but routine itself? Why not take a different path than the one that ends here?" Stacy got on defense again, wary of some attempt to get her pants off and raised an eyebrow. "A different path eh? That *might* not be a bad idea, depending on the path I guess." She smiled at him and left the conversation where it was, daring him to suggest something with her eyes as he smiled at her, unafraid of the silence. Growing a bit uncomfortable, Stacy broke and asked if he had anything in mind. "I do actually. It's possible to talk here, but the overall environment isn't really suited to deep conversation in my opinion, too loud, too much liquor and too many interruptions. Why don't we go to-" Stacy raised a hand slightly and shook her head sadly "Oh James, you were doing so well, so different at first, but now this? I'm looking for something *different*, not a quick lay!" James chuckled, a deep, pleasant sounding laugh that threw Stacy off guard. "Milady, you thoroughly wound me with your words and assumptions! Had you let me finish my sentence, you would have heard me invite you, not to my home or behind the bar, but to the coffee shop about ten minutes from here, where there's no liquor, no last call and no horrid music." Stacy went red and apologized, chiding herself for her impetuousness. "I'm so sorry James, I do have a tendency to jump ahead sometimes, that was rude of me." James waved his hand "Not at all, you've clearly been 'hunted' plenty of times, I'd be sick of it and wary of tricks and traps too. I just wanted a shot to get to know you as a person, nothing more. What do you say?" Stacy looked at her phone despite having nothing planned for the evening and nothing to do the next day either, glanced at Horace, who was trying to gently tell the two men she had been sitting between to lower their voices, then smiled. "Sure, let's go."

As soon as Stacy left the club, she began to get nervous. "What am I getting into?" She repeatedly thought to herself, along with a few other choice phrases, but before she could talk herself into turning around, almost on cue, her phone rang and James's deep, calm and confident voice pushed the fears out of her mind.

"Hello Stacy, I want to make sure you had no trouble finding the place."

"I'm fine, I mean it's fine, I'm close by."

"Is everything alright? You sound a bit nervous. Are you uncomfortable?

"Well, I said it was fine since the place was close and you seem like a really nice guy but...to be honest I am a bit nervous." Stacy felt relieved as saying what she felt but foolish as well, like she was wasting both of their time and leading him on in a cruel way that did neither of them any good, but was even more relieved when James answered.

"I completely understand, thank you for being honest with me. If you want to pick somewhere you are more comfortable with we could reschedule for tomorrow, or whenever you are available. I want you to be completely comfortable and-"

Stacy interjected "Then it's an acceptable sacrifice?"

"I don't think spending time with you is a sacrifice and I think a man pressuring an attractive young lady is a mark of lust, ineptitude and boorishness."

Stacy smiled and flushed a bit, feeling her cheeks grow warm as she decided to try to tease him, something she had done her whole life, starting with manipulating her father into buying her objects since he never had time to spend with her and moving on from there . She changed her tone to sound coquettish and coyly responded: "So lust isn't a good thing then? I don't make you feel lust?"

James chuckled deeply and sounded as calm as ever as he responded: "Stacy, when I first laid eyes on you tonight I could tell a few things about you. One of them was that you are indeed a very sexy woman, but would you like to know another thing I noticed?" Stacy was slightly taken aback, but curious as well "Certainly, what else did you notice?"

I noticed from your interactions that you are quite familiar with using, or some would say abusing your femininity to lead men on, tease them and otherwise have them behave in the manner you expect them to. Your flirtatious ways are the bait that draws that type of male in, your femininity is the snare and lust is the emotion that forms the leash you've held so many times before. I'm not bound by lust, so you can't control me with it. In fact, if I were to behave as you have in the past, I could abuse your natural curiosity to bait you, my masculinity to ensnare you and your own lust to control you, but I would rather deal with you as a person, not a prey item."

James was silent as a great many images ran through her mind, a large percentage of which were quite erotic in nature. She was so lost in her reverie that she didn't notice how long there had been silence on the other line and snapped back to reality when she heard a car starting in the distance.

"I'm on my way to the coffee shop now, will you be joining me?"

"Yes, I'd like that."

"Wonderful, I'll see you soon then. One more thing though."

"Yes?"

"During our conversation you interrupted me. Don't do that anymore, do I make myself clear young lady?"

As James finished his sentence, several things happened all at once. Stacy's cheeks went beet red, her eyes closed for a brief moment and she bit her lip to stifle the moan that threatened to escape her lips, a moan caused by her being incredibly aroused and not entirely sure why. As pleasure radiated through her she realized that James was still on the phone AND still awaiting an answer to his question.

"Um, sorry."

"Stacy, are you alright?"

"Of course, w...why wouldn't I be?"

"You sounded flustered; it appears that you've just discovered a fetish."

Stacy's jaw dropped and she was unable to speak from shock. Several seconds passed that felt like hours.

"Nonetheless I'll be at the coffee shop in ten minutes, should I await your arrival?"

"Ok...and yes."

"Yes?"

"Yes, you made yourself clear...about the interrupting."

"Good girl."

Stacy's nipples grew hard as soon as she heard that phrase and she excused herself before he was able to tell she was aroused again, biting her lip as she concentrated and drove on.

She reached the coffee shop soon after her conversation ended and drove around it three times to try to spot her fascinating new friend and calm down a bit Eventually she gave up on both things and called him.

"Yes?"

"I'm here, where are you?"

"In the back, I'll come and get you."

She wrung her hands in excitement with a tinge of worry, but those worries disintegrated as she saw him walking towards her with a smile. He was tall, taller than her by almost a foot and even more handsome in light that wasn't garish and flashing. He extended his hand and took hers, bringing it to his mouth and kissing it, making her blush anew as a woman at a table glowered at her for some reason. "A pleasure to see you again Stacy, you're even more beautiful in proper lighting. Right this way please." Stacy smiled at the glaring woman and followed James, giggling and doing a small curtsy when he pulled her chair out. He smiled bemusedly and spread his hands. "So, what will it be?" Stacy raised an eyebrow at the request and then laughed nervously. "Ummmm...I'm not quite sure..."

James folded his hands." Come on now, don't be shy. I could make a comment about how you clearly don't mind darker hues, but this is about what you want for yourself, don't let me influence you, speak from the heart!" Stacy Looked down and began to wring her hands a bit while she blushed. She didn't feel pressured, she felt aroused, but also embarrassed, which for some reason aroused her as well. James' smile soon faded and he looked at her in a stern manner, forcing her to hold his gaze without telling her to do so. As her cheeks brightened even more, almost to the level they had been at in the car. "Stacy, I don't have all night and neither do you, I need to know. Forget about everyone else here, forget about me too if it makes it easier for you, but I need to hear you say it, even if it's just a whisper." Stacy hoped he would push her too far but he held the tension where it was and left things up to her. She closed her eyes and looked down at her hands as she prepared to answer him. "I..... I think I have a......a fetish for-"

"A Fetish? For coffee?" James's smile had returned and the tension had evaporated. "I just want to know what you wanted to drink, what did you think I meant?" He stifled his laughter and touched Stacy's hand reassuringly as he stood up. "Don't look so mortified Stacy, just wanted to show you that teasing can indeed go both ways. I'm getting the chai latte, how about you?"

Stacy woke up and yawned, turning over the events from the previous night in her mind, going over every word exchanged, every touch, every sentence and fighting the urge to get excited, wanting to find something to make her wary, or better yet a reason to drop the whole thing and move on to the next. Whatever it was that she had with James, it was more than a rapport but less than a relationship, though not by much. She called her friend Cheryl and told her everything, from the first meeting at the club, to the first phone call to how she almost embarrassed herself, to the way they had talked for three hours without a break and aside from the mortifying revelation she nearly made, nothing remotely awkward had come up. Stacy told her she had never imagined herself being remotely interested in anyone so much older than her, but it made sense when she considered how boring, conformist and immature almost all of the men she had ever known around her age were. At 43 James was almost old enough to be her father, a fact Stacy tried and failed to push out of her head before it spawned any dirty thoughts. Even when the conversation had turned to sexuality, fetishes and kinks James hadn't said or done anything even remotely inappropriate, quite the opposite in fact, suggesting a few things for her to look up, a couple of books and several terms. "Well, what about after that? Did anything ELSE happen?" Cheryl asked expectantly. Stacy blushed and went on to tell her how after they had realized how early it was, they had left, with James walking Stacy to her car and giving her a polite kiss on the cheek, though as he did so his hand grabbed her ass, making her jump in surprise. She recalled the feeling of his hand, confident and firm and the way he didn't apologize for himself afterward, but told her that he would really like to see her again. After that, despite herself she had pulled him in for a kiss that was quite a bit more than the one he had given her at first and she recalled the way he had growled and went with it, backing her up against her car as he kissed her deeply, his hands again grabbing her ass, pulling her deeper into the kiss until he broke it and said that he would *really* really like to see her again, adjusting his slacks as he did. Cheryl sounded slightly annoyed somehow when she finally spoke. "Great job, I should go to clubs and be bored, maybe I'll meet a nice fellow. Can you teach me how to do that bored rich girl act?"

Stacy was insulted more by her friends tone than the comment. "*You* make more than I do!" She said. "Big deal, I don't have a rich daddy. I've gotta go, tell me when the wedding is." She said before she hung up abruptly.

Having nobody else to talk to about it, she decided to call her father. The phone rang once, twice and she knew he was reading the display and frowning, then hoping it would get disconnected before five rings. Since it didn't, he answered, sounding nervous and unsure, like he was talking to a police officer who had stopped him: "Ahem, hello there d..dear...Stacy my dear. How is my girl?

She grimaced at his unfamiliarity and sighed. "Hi Daddy, I was wondering if I could stop by today and spend some time with you?" She felt eager to talk to him about something more in depth than how her car was doing or if she needed money followed by a hasty retreat once he had paid her off. He sighed, a special sigh that conveyed the image of him shrugging helplessly and apologetically all at once.

"I have a relationship situation that I would like to get your input on. "A relationship situation," Stacy's father asked dumbfounded. "Are you pregnant?" "No, of course not" Stacy snapped into the phone. "Oh, have you met a nice boy and thinking about settling down?" "No Dad, I'm not getting hitched anytime soon."

"Oh, well I'm the guy you call about business, not relationship advice. That's not really my area of expertise. Don't you have some girlfriends you can talk to?" Stacy sighed and realized this phone call was a bad idea. She spoke calmly, almost jovially as if it wasn't a big deal anymore, as she did when she was angry. "You know what? It's fine. You're right. I'll call one of my girlfriends or just figure it out on my own. I don't know what I was thinking by bothering you with my relationship problems. Stacy heard a sigh of relief on the other end of the line. "That's my girl! I hate to cut this call short but I have another call coming in. I'll send you some money so you can buy something pretty for your next date. Love you."

Stacy was torn between crying, yelling, or breaking something, but in the end she did none of these things. She called James, then hung up midway through and sent him a text: "Can you meet me at the coffee shop please? I've had a rough morning."

"I happen to already be here."

When Stacy arrived, she saw James outside at one of the tables with a cup and a muffin. He smiled at her and headed her way. He took her hand briefly while walking with her to his table and she resisted the urge to hug him, but before they sat down he wrapped his arm around her shoulder and squeezed her briefly. It didn't feel at all sexual and relieved some of her tension and apprehension about discussing what she was about to with him.

"Well, no need to hold back, who or what got your feathers ruffled this morning?

Stacy sighed, sat back and then looked away with uncertainty. She decided to just speak from the heart and clenched her hands. "I like you, but I don't know about dating someone older than me. I called my dad but he blew me off, as always, and my girlfriend sounded either angry or jealous or something.

James held a hand up, making Stacy raise an eyebrow as anger swelled inside of her, that familiar feeling of being pushed off to the side, not taken seriously.

She glared at him, but then softened as he lowered his hand before speaking.

"Stacy, I don't mean to interrupt you but I like you too." James touched her hand softly and Stacy felt a jolt of electricity surge through her entire body.

"Your honesty is beautiful but between your friend and your father which one angered you the most?" Stacy shrugged. "Oh come on now, surely your friend's insincerity didn't bother you as much as your fathers?" With a smile she admitted that it didn't. James smiled, took her hand and commanded her attention with his gaze.

"Stacy you're the youngest girl I've ever considered pursuing, but I've already determined at least to try. Just from the way you carry yourself I know you aren't an average woman."

"I'm sorry your relationship with your father is strained but if it's any comfort, mine is as well so my empathy is real." "As for your girlfriend, I'd just let it go if at all possible." James shrugged his broad shoulders and squeezed her hand slightly before letting it go, though she grabbed it again as she shook her head with a smile. "Hey, if I didn't know any better I'd think you were going to give me a chance!" He said with a grin. Stacy returned his grin and then lowered her voice as she slid her calf alongside his under the table "Why don't we go back to your place and finish what we started last time?"

James walked her out of the coffee shop and to her car. He looked deeply and longingly into her eyes. "I'd love to take you home but you are vulnerable right now and I don't want to take advantage of that, you know?" It was now her turn to grab his ass as she pulled him into her, kissing him deeply. "Then follow me to my place and help me to not feel this way?" James smiled and promised to do what he could and they kissed once more before getting into their separate cars. Stacy led the way and was quite glad it would be a short drive to her place.

After all the anger of the morning and then relief of getting it off her chest, Stacy was exhausted, though it was far more mental and emotional in nature than anything else. As soon as they were inside her apartment James led her to her couch and began massaging her shoulders with his large, warm hands, making her moan as he spoke. "There's not a thing for you to worry about my dear, you just lay here and enjoy your massage, it is my duty to make you feel as refreshed as I can." Stacy smiled and stretched out a bit, feeling the tension in her shoulders begin to leave as James' huge hands caressed and kneaded down her shoulders, her arms and then further down her back, stopping just above the hem of her jeans. He swatted her ass softly a few times. "Lose the jeans." He said authoritatively, making Stacy blush and whimper slightly as she obeyed him. She slid her hand under her and unbuttoned the tight, low rise jeans and started wiggling out of them before she was held by his left hand as his right did the rest of the work for her, peeling the jeans off smoothly, leaving her in only her panties, a black thong that was beginning to grow damp in the front. James ignored the dampening thong and continued his massage, skillfully working each of her thighs, down to her calves, then her ankles before doing each of her toes, starting with the smallest and spending a full minute on each one. He rubbed the top, then to the sole of her foot, the instep, the heel and then went back up her other leg, doing the process in reverse, starting with her toes and ending with her thigh. "Mmmmmmmm...James..." Stacy moaned as his hands squeezed both of her thighs together, working heat into her muscles that radiated into her crotch as well, increasing her arousal until she reached back and tried to pull her thong to one side, hoping to get his attention to shift from massaging her outsides to giving her an internal treatment. She whimpered as her hand was swatted away and then did so again as his right hand which had just been so tender and gentle to her skin now came down sharply against it, making her grow in wetness as she cried out in surprise. "This is massage time, you just lay there and let me take care of you, understand? Stay there, don't move, understand?" He said firmly. "Okay..." Was her first reply to him, but she then felt another swat on her ass and she bit her lip before answering breathlessly "Yes Sir", blushing and feeling excited at his commanding tone. He began kissing her softly, starting at her ear, trailing them down her back, over her ass cheeks and down her legs as he worked her flesh with his hands, their warmth and firm pressure invigorating her. "You're quite tense, but I'm making some progress here. Did you look up the terms I mentioned?" She nodded silently as she stretched out, feeling the muscles in her legs loosen up as her masseur turned her onto her side, pressing into her from behind as he continued massaging her as he took his shirt and shorts off. "I'm going to play a little game with you, since I know you enjoy teasing I think you'll quite enjoy some teasing being done to you. Don't speak, just listen to the words I'm going to say to you and answer me with your body." He said as he licked her ear, making her shudder and nod emphatically. "First...Controlled." He growled to her, feeling her moan without opening her mouth as she pressed herself back against him. "I see, that's a yes...Next is...Groped." As he said it he squeezed her breasts and lightly kissed the nape of her neck, feeling her nipples harden even more at his touch. "Another yes...now...penetration?" At this she moaned aloud, then stopped herself as she heard him chuckle and rub his fully erect cock between her thighs. "Good girl, ready for an internal massage?" She nodded and rolled onto her stomach, feeling herself grow even wetter with anticipation.

She felt him pressing into her from behind and soon his hand pulled her thong to one side and his thick cock slid in easily, lubricated by her wetness. She felt him sliding up into her, deep inside her as he continued the massage on the outside, kneading her buns as he flexed his thick dick inside of her. "You feel amazing Stacy...so...hot..wet...tight!" He said between groans and thrusts. Stacy nodded, unable to speak from the pleasure as she tried not to cry out. Soon she felt James' cock twitch, but instead of going faster he slowed down as he took in a deep breath and his dick stopped twitching as he continued to pump in and out of her. "You can cum if you want, but I'm not going to just yet, this is a massage for you, so I'm going to make it last, don't mind my breathing work back here, cum as you please." Stacy felt the warmth building within her as James' hands moved around to her tits, cupping them and tweaking her nipples as she laid there and enjoyed the wonderful feeling of being worked on, taken and taken care of all at once by him. His mouth on the nape of her neck, his large hands squeezing her breasts and playing with her nipples, using the perfect combination of tenderness and roughness, his weight pressing onto her, trapping her though she wouldn't have escaped if she could have and his hard, hot cock thrusting into her again and again. She felt her first orgasm rising, not just from her pussy, but from her core, melting away her tiredness along with the massage and filling her with pleasure until her mind went white and she cried out, pressing her face into the pillow and screaming in bliss as the massive orgasm overtook her and made her muscles spasm as she lost her breath. When it began to subside she felt James still within her, still massaging her from the inside as his hands traveled down her back and grabbed her ass cheeks, spreading them as she moaned, her voice only just coming back. "Shh..., I want you to cum for me once more, than perhaps you can rest." He ran a large finger down the crack of her shapely ass and rubbed her anus repeatedly, teasing it. At first she shook her head, but as he continued the pleasure overcame her embarrassment and she groaned as she went wild and thrust back at him, trying to take him deeper, faster. He swatted her ass sharply and licked her ear before whispering to her, somehow with more force than if he had shouted it: "Nope, be a good girl and stay still for me. I will be the one making you cum, understand? This is my orgasm, I'm giving it to you and you are to take it. Stay still." She felt all desire to move leave her as if someone had flipped a switch and she went limp, feeling exhausted despite the relief flooding through her. She felt his finger enter her ass slowly, agonizingly slowly before being joined by a second one, stretching her out with lovely girth as they probed deep into her, soon meeting the rhythm of his cock and matching it as she recalled one of the terms she had looked up without it being suggested "Oh James...yes...double..." She moaned, feeling his cock swell somehow as he growled and bit her ear softly, sending a shiver through her entire being. "Yessss, double what? Say it, tell me what I'm doing to you or I won't let you cum." She blushed despite herself and felt the orgasm beginning even as she cried out, obeying him as it overtook her. "Double penetrati-" was as far as she got before her entire body began to shake and she bit the pillow to avoid screaming as both of her holes began to clench around their invaders, milking his cock and pulling an orgasm from him despite his words earlier, forcing him to cum as he had done to her and making him groan loudly before collapsing onto the bed beside her, turning her back to him and wrapping his arms around her waist as he massaged her cheeks with his softening cock and panting to regain his strength. "I didn't want to cum, but you...kind of made me...that's never happened before. She smiled and snuggled into his arms. He kissed her neck softly and she could hear the smile in his voice as he spoke "Well, how about we stay like this for a while, then go again to celebrate?" She smiled but before she could nod her phone began to play her text message sound. She checked it and saw it was a notification from her bank that her father had transferred some money into her account. James asked "Do you have to take care of something?" Stacy turned the phone off, tossed it away and leaned back against him with a grin. "Yes, I need to help you with that celebration round in a little while!"

BOOK 2: SPANKED BEHIND THE LIBRARY

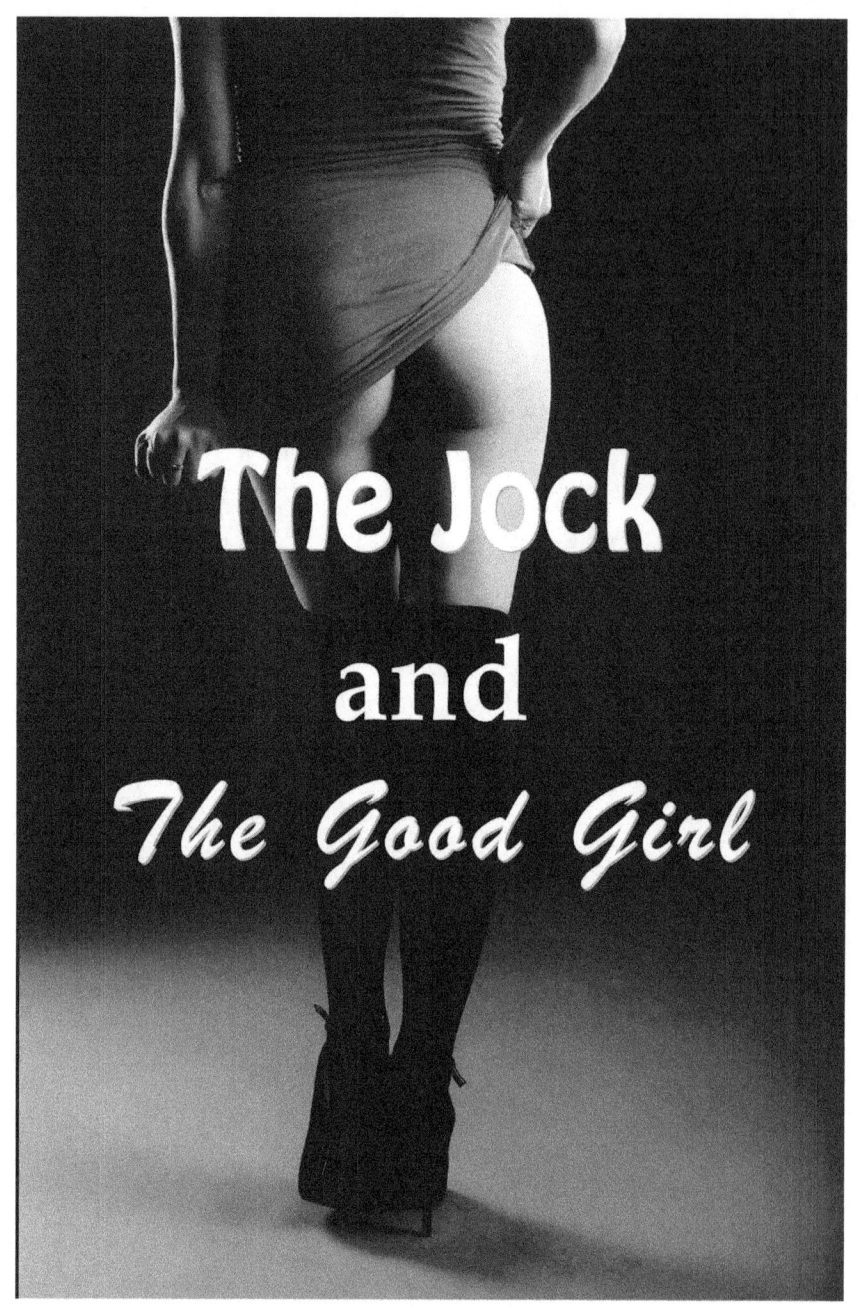

After getting both the first and best massage she ever had received, Stacy sat near James as he recovered his strength for the "celebration round" he had promised her. "What are you doing so far away from me? Come here." He said, taking her hand and pulling her onto him as she giggled and blushed yet again. Her mind was awash with feelings, all of them positive, some so much so that it made her nervous. She thought about how just a few days ago she hadn't even known this man, yet here he was in her house, on her couch, holding her naked body against his and she couldn't have been happier.

"So what do you do for work James?"

"I'm a freelance web developer and graphic artist. I also have some smaller businesses on the side. What about you?"

"I have a job at an office, but my dad pays for my place and stuff."

"I thought your relationship with him wasn't so good?"

"It's not; he basically pays me to leave him alone. Every time I talk to him he buys me something to end the conversation early, he's always been that way. My mom had an affair right under his nose for over a year and he either didn't know or just didn't care, and when she left he didn't even notice for a week. I stayed because I wasn't invited along with her and her new lover, but I would have anyhow, I was a precocious, spoiled brat. I was terrible in grade school and misbehaved so much I got home schooled for all of middle school, it was so boring I got my dad to agree to send me back to real school if I straightened my grades, so I did. In high school I first started manipulating other guys the same way I imagined I was manipulating my father. Then I went to college and majored in sociology, graduated and got a job at an office, answering phones for one of the companies my dad owns. He agreed to get me the job after I got into a bit of trouble once I graduated and had nothing to do but party and drink, among other things. Are you bored to tears yet, listening to a spoiled child whine about her first world problems?"

James smiled "No, not at all. In fact, I just got a great idea."

"What is it?"

James leaned back "I want you to tell me all about the guys you played in college."

Stacy began to feel heat at the outer edge of her face as James strong arms squeezed her lightly, urging her onward. She looked down despite James being behind her and started speaking in a very quiet voice that was tinged with arousal.

"Well, there was a guy in my American History class. He was a loud, obnoxious and extroverted type. I think he was on the football team. He flirted with me constantly during class, and eventually the professor put us on a team together with another student, a middle aged single mother. She never had time to come to the library for the study sessions and I would flirt with him as we studied, I wanted to see if I could get him to do my paper for me. I knew the material; I just wanted to see if I could get him to do it. He told me he would just get his done by a writing service and I asked if he would have them do mine too. I told him I would pay him back whatever it cost but he said it was fine as long as he got my number and a lunch in exchange…I said yes, turned in the paper and then tested out of the class." She said, putting her face into her hands as warm redness spread from her cheeks to her neck and James noticed this and kissed her shoulder blade softly. "Why does that embarrass you now though?" He said as he ran his hands up and down her sides slowly. "It's just…I shouldn't have done it, I know that now, but I knew it *then* too, I just wanted to feel in control, it made me feel good to make him do just what I wanted him to. Like I said earlier, my dad was where I learned how to manipulate men and I had become good at it. It was a juvenile thing to do, but it *was* fun, as bad as that sounds." James pulled her back towards him, his hardening cock pressing against her and making her gasp as he spoke into her ear. "Why don't we re-create that event, but with a twist?"

Stacy couldn't nod her head quickly enough. James chuckled and sighed, changing position on the couch so that he now had his legs spread with Stacy still in his lap. She grew shy and embarrassed again and tried to scoot off of his lap to grab a blanket but he chuckled and held her fast and licked her ear, making a shiver of pure sensation lance through her body. "Don't be such a prude, you have nothing that needs covering. Every part of you is beautiful." Let's talk about how we're going to create that scene. It will start in a library of course, I'll be the guy, but I'm going to be improvising, you can of course be yourself, no need to act." He said with a wink as he massaged her breasts, tweaking her hardened nipples as he nuzzled her neck, inhaling deeply. "You got so hot when you described teasing that jock, but it's going to be the other way around when we do it for real, I'm not going to be me, I'm going to be him, you know? If you call me James I won't have a clue who you're talking about. If you absolutely have to stop things for some reason, say-" Stacy shook her head with a smile, making the one James already wore grow even wider. "No safe word? You're a risk taker aren't you? I love it! This is going to be so much fun; I promise you'll enjoy it. We can do this sort of thing as often as you want to; it never gets old if you ask me. Variety and imagination make everything better." He said as he kissed down her neck to the top of her shoulder, then into the indentation of her collarbone. Stacy hoped he meant that the role-play session would take place the next day and honestly would have jumped at the chance to do it right then, but James answered her as if he read her mind. "Give me three days to prepare for it, I'm going to check out the library and get into character, I know that might be a while to wait but trust me, the anticipation is part of the fun as well." She nodded; feeling so aroused from between his kisses and caresses that adding the thought of their session in three days' time had her aching with need. She turned and kissed James deeply, pressing her tongue into his mouth and exploring it as she rolled her hips and ground herself against his rigid, throbbing cock. Soon he grabbed her hips and pulled her forward, angling her so that her lips slid up and down the length of his cock, sending waves of electric pleasure through both of them as they moaned, never unlocking their lips. The need Stacy had felt aching within her threatened to consume her entirely if it wasn't taken care of soon and through kisses she breathlessly whimpered as she tried to impale herself on him but was held fast as he changed position again, leaning back and then sliding her upwards until she was positioned above him, her excitement leaking onto him as she dropped herself on him, her earlier shyness was long gone. At the moment of connection the two of them gasped aloud, James holding her shapely ass as Stacy dug her nails into his arms to keep from crying out. From her position on top Stacy could set the pace and began rolling her hips as she rose and fell, feeling him thrusting up to meet her as pleasure coursed through the both of them. Whereas before James was dominant and took the lead, now he acquiesced and allowed Stacy to control the depth and pacing himself slightly surprised by how intensely she was riding him. He moved his hands to her hips and held on tight as he thrust upwards into her again and again, watching her breasts heaving as sweat beaded on both of their bodies from the exertion. Soon Stacy quickened her pace as she drew nearer and nearer to another climax, her third despite this being her first session with James. He felt her approaching release and held her fast as he began furiously pounding into her, making her writhe and throw her head back as she passed the point of no return and felt her orgasm welling up within her. "Stacy, look at me. I want you to look into my eyes as you cum." James told her as he stared unflinchingly into her eyes, his gaze transfixing her as his hips drove ever deeper and she focused on the feeling of indescribable warmth and pleasure rising up from her core and radiating throughout her body, her vision clouding as she kept her eyes locked onto his until she slumped onto his chest, feeling his strong hands stroking her back as she tried to catch her breath.

Stacy's excitement had only increased each day that their "live fire" role-play session drew closer and on the morning it was to take place she was barely able to eat anything and sat around watching the clock and huffing because of the cruel way time went slowest when waiting on something fun. Her drive to the library passed in the blink of an eye and as she got out, the tall brick building took on a new air to her, no longer was it a stuffy, boring place to go and study, but a playground for fantasies.

She went inside expecting to see James sitting somewhere obvious, but she didn't see him at all. The lobby was essentially empty save the few receptionists, so she went up the stairs hurriedly to the next level. Upon reaching it she walked around the entire room, looking between the shelves and glancing at people reading things to see if any matched James' body type, but saw nobody. She thought about calling him, but decided against it, she was enjoying herself and wanted to make it last. She decided to take the elevator up to the third floor and as she got in, she saw him: He was dressed in a pink T-shirt and jeans with a letterman jacket on over it and had a baseball cap on, completing the look quite effectively. Stacy's eyes widened as he smirked, the doors starting to close until she got her bearings and hit the door open button, holding the elevator for her study partner. He strutted into the elevator and nodded, then smiled wide as he "recognized" her. "Oh HEY! It's you, from class! About time you got here, I've been waiting! You look great!" Stacy giggled and shook his hand. "You look totally different James, well played." She said, prompting her partner to give her an odd look. "Who the heck is James? I'm Joe, you know, from class? We DO have a project together right?" Stacy caught on and realized the meaning of the text she got upon entering the library

"(Stay in character or you get a penalty)"

They made it to the third floor, walked over to a table and sat down, not pulling out her chair as James had already gotten her used to being done for her. She harrumphed at him and stood, tapping her heel and looking expectantly at him, a look he responded to with a blank stare. "Is your chair dirty or something?" Stacy shook her head defiantly. "Pull it out for me, I'm a lady!"

Joe chuckled "Yeah well, you ain't MY lady, so sit your preppy ass down and let's do this project."

Stacy blushed and complied, realizing she forgot her books. "Joe…I…"

"Forgot your books eh? You do that in class too, come sit on this side and we'll share." Stacy got up and moved to the other side of the desk where James leaned back and patted his lap.

"Ugh, real charming." Stacy said, sitting next to him and scooting the chair a bit further from him and his crudeness.

"I'm a star football player, what do you expect? Anyhow, why aren't you a cheerleader? With an ass like yo-"

"Joe!" Stacy hissed "Stop it, let's just study and get this over with!" Despite her exasperation she soon felt herself growing flushed at his constant rudeness, lack of care and needlessly rough manner. He didn't seem to be going out of his way to be rude; it was more like he didn't know any other way to behave. "Sheesh, fine! I was just complimenting you! Let's do the vocabulary test first I guess, I'll give it to you and then you can do me after that." Stacy rolled her eyes again at his uncouth manner and the words he had chosen. He smiled and cleared his throat, then began.

"Okay, first word is...arousal. Define it or spell it then we'll go to the next one." Stacy went red and looked down, wringing her hands as her embarrassment battled valiantly against her own arousal but found that the two feelings soon stopped fighting and joined forces, leaving her more aroused than before as well as embarrassed at her feelings and how they betrayed her so quickly. Joe tapped the table impatiently. "Come on Stacy, this is an easy one. You don't get a chance to do me unless you get five in a row." Stacy couldn't bring herself to look up and whispered her answer. "A....arousal: A-r-o-u-s-a-l" Joe nodded and looked at the list again. "Next up: Sensual." Stacy felt her breathing quicken slightly as Joe nudged her foot under the table. "Sensual: S-e-n-s-u-a-l" Joe nodded and turned a page. "Alright, enough easy stuff, time to give you something longer and harder than before, this one's a mouthful so take your time with it, no need to rush, just take it bit by bit, a little at a time...Sadomasochism." Stacy was torn between making a wry comment and trying to actually spell the word, but soon chose the former. "Are you sure that's the vocabulary list from class?" Joe nodded. "Nice try, but you've still gotta spell it." Stacy sighed and pushed away Joe's foot, as it was making it even harder for her to concentrate as it slid up and down her calves. "Sadomasochism: S-a-d-o-m-a-s-o-c-i-s-m. Happy now?" She said with a smirk. Joe *did* indeed look happy. "I am, you misspelled your word, so you get two more tries before...well I won't spoil the surprise, but do you want to try again or have a different word?" Stacy huffed and accepted a different word, having always hated to lose or make a mistake at anything as Joe chose a new term from the long list while again rubbing his foot up her leg underneath the table, making her turn a slightly deeper red as she stifled a moan. "Alright, here's an easy one: Areolae. Would you like the definition?" Stacy bit her lip as his foot rose higher than before, stroking the inside of her thigh as she shook her head. "Are you sure? It's a tricky word, you might want to err on the side of caution and let me define it for you." Stacy closed her eyes and visualized the word as she spelled it out.

"Areola: A-r-e-o-l-a." Joe shook his head with mock sadness and showed her the word. "I gave you a chance Stacy, it was the *plural* form of the word, meaning it had an extra 'e' on the end."

Stacy was aghast and clenched her fists. "You tricked me James!" This elicited another quizzical look from her study partner. "I keep telling you, I don't have a clue who this James is. Might he be your boyfriend? Would he get upset seeing you here, sitting so close to a fellow like me?" Stacy giggled and tried to take the list from Joe, but he pulled it away and instead kissed her lightly on the nose, making her blush furiously and pull away, clamming up and honestly feeling a bit like she was betraying James and going behind his back as her study partner chuckled. "That answers my previous question quite succinctly. Now, last try before you get a...punishm-I mean penalty. Here we go, the word is: Cunnilingus. Take your time with it, it took me a while to master it myself, don't rush and focus fully on it, block out everything else." He said as his free hand crept around Stacy's back and moved to the hem of her jeans, trying to work its way inside. Stacy was more aroused than she had ever been in her life from the scenario and the taboo of being in public so the addition of Joe and his large hand persistently trying to feel her up with no regard for her squirming and protests drove her over the edge and made her have a small orgasm right then and there, biting her lip and arching her back as the waves of pleasure radiated throughout her body, soon settling and renewing her embarrassment. She squirmed around until she managed to free herself from Joe and his wandering hand, then exhaled slowly and started spelling. "C-u-n-" Joe shook his head and interrupted her.

"You know the proper protocol for spelling a word. State the word, and then spell it. This is your last shot before you get a penalty, so I suggest you do it by the book young lady." Stacy looked down and wrung her hands as the familiar feelings grew within her, arousal and nervousness intertwining and feeding off of one another as Joe sternly stared at her, forbidding her from looking away. She met his gaze and steeled herself as she realized that she quite wanted to see what the penalty was, then started spelling once again. "C...Cunnilingus: K-u-n-n-i-l-i-n-g-u-s" Joe smiled wide and then shook his head as he stood up and told her to do the same with his commanding gaze. "That was your last shot, too bad for you. Come with me, it's time for your penalty now."

Joe and Stacy walked side by side through the library with a deliberately slow pace, Stacy was squirming in anticipation and trying to hurry ahead, but Joe kept the pace with a smile. He was enjoying every second of this, leading her to the penalty that she chose herself, her curiosity winning out over the nervousness at what it might be. She truly felt like she was dealing with a different man, from the way he was dressed, his overbearing cologne and extroverted personality to the way he held her arm possessively, as if she might break and run at any moment. Every time they encountered stairs he prodded her ahead of him, feeling his eyes on her rear as they descended, making it out of the library after what seemed like an hour of walking. Joe then tugged her arm again, the two of them heading around the back of the large building as Stacy grew even more nervous and aroused at sneaking about in broad daylight and finally spoke: "Alright, enough suspense, what is this penalty? I thought you were going to make me have lunch with you or something, but this is-" Joe shushed her and led her further behind the library and up toward the red brick exterior, pushing her slightly towards it. "This is your punishment right here, put your hands on the wall." Stacy raised an eyebrow questioningly at him but he stepped closer and she decided to go along with it rather than seeing how far he would take his rough and crude character act. "Good girl, both hands. Yeah, stick your ass out more." He put both of his large hands on her waist and forced her to arch her back, grabbing her ass and chuckling as he pressed his body against hers and whispered into her ear. "I've been wanting to do this to you since we met in class, think you can get whatever you want by huffing and puffing, pouting and acting like a little brat eh? This is what brats deserve." Stacy tried to form words but her breath caught in her throat as she was put into position, feeling more exposed and more aroused every second. She bit her lip as she saw him raise his hand out of the corner of her eye and then closed them, waiting for the impact.

WHACK!

"Good girl, keep quiet and take your punishment."

SMACK!

"Two down, three to go."

WHAP!

"I bet you'll take our next study session more seriously now."

SLAP!

"Almost done, one more whack on this nice little ass of yours."

WHACK!

"There, that's just what you deserve for your behavior. Next time we have a study session I want you to carefully study the vocabulary words beforehand, definitions too. You look really hot right now, if I didn't have practice in a while you'd probably end up cheating on whoever 'James' is, but I've gotta run. I'll catch you later."

After that abrupt departure following the penalty, Stacy was charged up with no outlet, at least for the moment. She walked slowly to her car and gingerly sat down, feeling a bit of soreness already on her rear, though she found it wasn't entirely unpleasant, it felt similar to the soreness she often felt after a good workout, a reminder that she had done something she didn't do every day. Soon her phone rang and she heard the smile in James' voice as she answered. "Hey Stacy, how's your day been?"

"It's been wonderful so far, but I'd really like to tell you about it in person, where are you?"

"I'm just finishing up a little side project, want to meet at the coffee place and chat?"

"No...How about my place? Or yours, whichever is closer."

"Hmm? I don't know. I have a lot of work to catch up on."

"James!"

"You know I'm just messing with you baby, sit tight."

Stacy waited a few moments after the call ended, considered calling him back, but soon a knock on her window made her jump a bit, then she smiled as she let James in. He had a large duffel bag with him and was back to looking like his normal self from head to toe. He got in and smiled at her briefly before she pounced on him, pressing him into the seat as she pressed her tongue deeply into his mouth, taking him quite by surprise with her forwardness and passion. A few seconds after his initial "Mmmph!" he got into the swing of things, becoming aroused himself and matching her fire, their making out turning briefly into a pseudo wrestling match as he grabbed her ass and pulled her onto him after letting the seat back and sliding it rearward, giving them plenty of legroom. He felt her hands roaming his body, one snaking its way up under his shirt and pinching his right nipple as she nipped his bottom lip, making him groan as she sucked the damage and fondled his balls through his pants. He tried to unfasten her bra from the back, but found her to be moving around too much and ended up just pulling it down in front, freeing her breasts and exposing them to his hands as she nodded, their first kiss unbroken as he felt her hard nipples and tugged them upwards, feeling her whimper into his mouth.

James soon spoke as his hands continued feeling all over every inch of Stacy, mentioning that the library would be closing soon and they would almost certainly be seen with her parked where she was. "Let's go back to my place and finish up what we've got going here. I may as well ride with you, that way I can keep a hand on you all the way back." He said with a grin. The entire short drive back to James apartment was filled with events that kept them both quite aroused, neither of them bothered to fix their clothes and at the first stop sign, James reached over and pulled down the zipper of her jeans, making her gasp as he did so and smile impishly when she tried to re-zip and he lightly pushed her hand away. "Stay like that for me; you look so hot that way." After that, at the third red light on the path to their destination Stacy did the same thing to James, freeing his erection from his pants through the fly and stroking it briefly before the light changed color and they set off once more. When they arrived at James apartment complex, he had Stacy park in back under the car port. "Hey my apartment is right there, let's run to the door like we are right now!" James said as Stacy turned off her car, taking her hand before she could try to zip up. She bit her lip and looked at the distance between the car and the apartment, then down at the state both of them were in. Her jeans were unzipped and the front of her pink thong was exposed, but James was in a far further state of undress as his thick cock was proudly standing up, the shaft sticking lewdly out of his pants, somehow more erotic because they were still up all the way. His belt was also undone but none of this seemed to perturb him in the least. If it had been just her who was being asked to get out in such a state she never would have done it. But she felt as if her and James were partners in crime and squeezed his hand as she nodded and opened her door. The walk from the car to the door took only nine seconds, but Stacy could feel her heart pounding in her chest as they reached their destination and was blushing deeply, though it was mitigated by her arousal at James and his seeming indifference. He didn't look nervous in the least and unlocked his door with calm, measured movements, even the short walk to the door had taken him longer than it had Stacy, who ran as if she was being chased. Once he unlocked the door and they were finally inside Stacy flopped down onto the massive beanbag he had in the center of his room and felt a bit tired from the sheer level of excitement that she had been at ever since the roleplaying session began a couple of hours ago. "You look tired Stacy, are you alright?" James asked as he took his jeans off and folded them over the back of his large recliner, his cock at half-staff. Some of Stacys previous shyness returned at seeing James walking about so freely as he was and she blushed, looking away with a giggle of embarrassment as he laid down next to her on the beanbag, putting his arms around her waist and kissing her as he tugged her jeans downward.

"Why don't you tell me about your day? You seemed really…charged up somehow, is there any particular reason?" Stacy let herself relax into the arms that embraced her and closed her eyes, thinking back on her study session and replaying the events in her mind's eye as James' large hands worked their magic on her, making the arousal rise in her body as she felt it do the same in her mind. "James...I never told you about the second study session I had with that guy, the one I mentioned to you a few days ago." James did a perfect job of pretending to think back for a few seconds before recalling the event in question. "Ah, the jock? I didn't know you ever saw him again after the first session, how did it go?" She melted into his arms as his hands kneaded her shoulders and she continued. "It was okay I guess, I didn't really study for the vocabulary test and so when he quizzed me on the words I got most of them wrong." She moaned as his hands worked their way under her shirt, massaging her sides as she raised her arms and let him slide the shirt up and off in one quick motion, not even interrupting her story. "I guess he got upset at me for wasting his time, so he said if I got one more wrong I'd get a penalty." James stopped massaging for a fraction of a second, then continued, working her breasts and tracing his fingers around the smooth flesh surrounding them before rubbing inward.

"A penalty? That sounds a bit strange, did you tell him that since he wasn't really your teacher he therefore couldn't penalize you?" He said as he rolled her hard nipples between his thumb and forefinger, eliciting a moan from her as she shook her head. "No...Oh James...I want...I wanted to see what the penalty was! I spelled the last word wrong on purpose!" She said, actually hiding her face with her hands as the embarrassment outmatched her arousal for a brief moment before James' kisses to her neck and insistent tugging on her nipples restored the balance. "That's not like you at all...what a bad girl you were. Well, what was the last word you misspelled?" She turned and kissed his ear, whispering it to him. "It was...cunnilingus. I spelled it with a K and then...I got the penalty." James had ceased using his hands on her nipples and was now licking them, alternating between each one as his hands went lower, pulling her panties to the side and letting him feel her wetness. "Mmhm, what was it? Tell me what he did to you, and don't leave anything out." He said sternly as she stretched out, letting him kiss down her stomach to the source of her wetness, licking around her outer lips while he squeezed her ass firmly. "He...spanked me out behind the library. He made me...mmmm... lean against the wall and stick my rear end out, then he spanked me five times and left, that's all.

Nothing else happened James, I promise." She said as let out the moans she had held back during her story. "I see...Nothing wrong with that I suppose, you *did* spell the words wrong and you let him do it, jocks will be jocks I suppose. I don't blame him for wanting to get a hand on this ass of yours really, too bad for him though; he doesn't get to do things to it like I do." He said as he came up for air, still massaging her cheeks while staring intently at her. She soon had her head back as he licked deep into her folds and then back up to her engorged clitoris, sucking and stroking it with his tongue as his fingers worked their way deeper into her as she shuddered. He sucked harder and found her g-spot, rubbing it as he began lashing her clit harder than before, making her go wild and grab his hair, pushing him deeper as she cried out in ecstasy. She felt her orgasm approaching quickly and squeezed her legs together, losing herself in the pure passion that was beginning to boil over from inside of her, the sensations from her g-spot merging with the waves emanating from her clitoris and combining before washing over her, making her mind temporarily go blank as she screamed out in total satisfaction.

The first thing she became aware of was James moving his head around and pushing her thighs a bit, making her blush as she let him go and he sat back gasping, though he was still smiling. "Well, I guess there's no need to ask if you enjoyed that!" She hugged him tightly and leaned onto him.

"Absolutely...can we do that again sometime?" He chuckled and stroked her hair. "Oh you can be certain that we will, and soon. Next week however, I get to choose the scenario!"

BOOK 3: TOTAL ROLE-PLAY

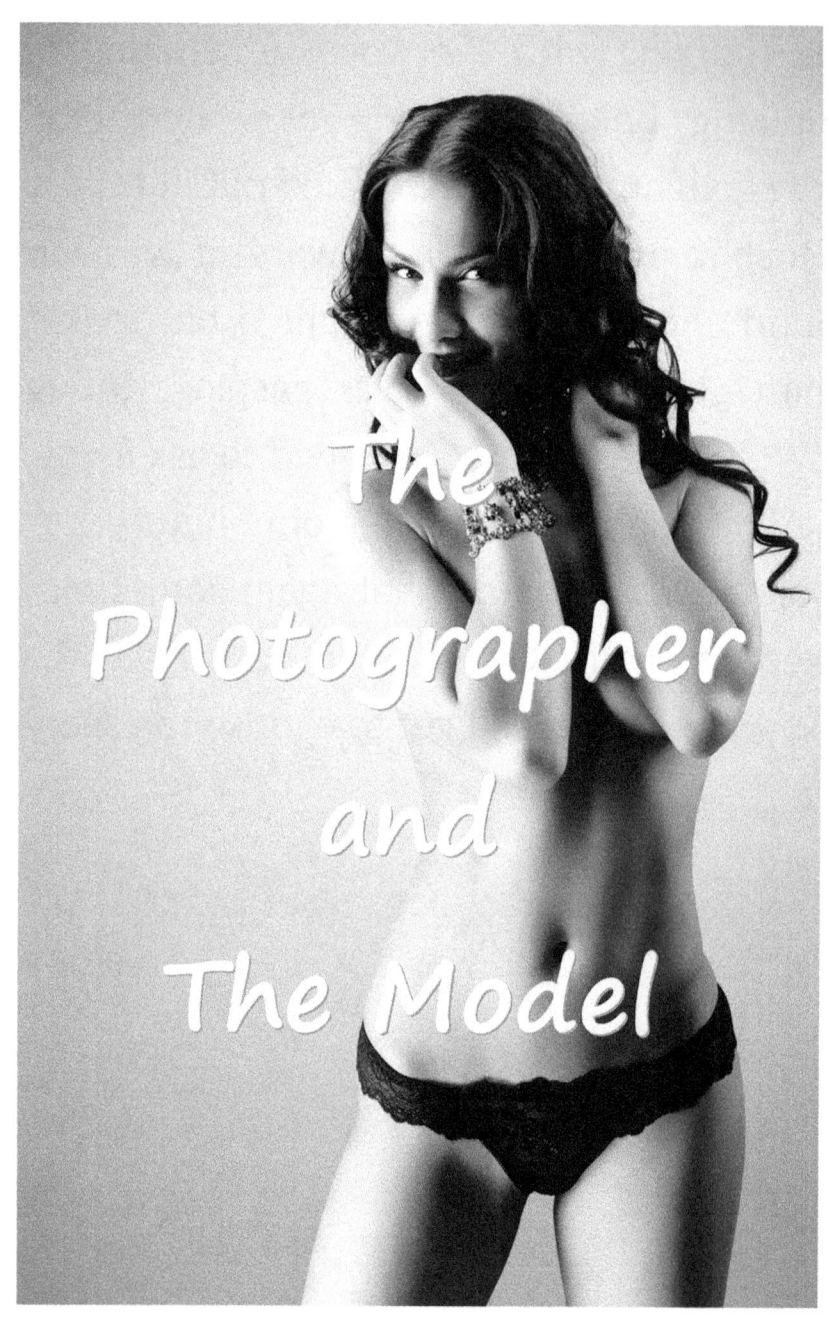

The morning after Stacy and James' first foray into what he called "Total Role-play" dawned, the sun rising and casting it's light upon the two of them sleeping soundly, James with his arms wrapped firmly around her waist. He awoke first, yawning and spending a few moments laying there silently while smiling and enjoying each passing second, not thinking about the night before or the day to come. He seized every single nuance of each passing second, the light filtering into his apartment through his window and the way it played off of her hair, the warmth of her body so close to his, her scent and the smoothness of her naked flesh. After they had made love the two of them fell asleep immediately, the day's activities leaving them totally fulfilled rather than exhausted. Soon Stacy began to stir, moaning happily as James pulled her closer to him, hastening her awakening. She turned to face him and pressed her head into his chest and then smiling at him, looking as happy as he felt.

"Good morning babe, I was going to ask how you were feeling this morning but I can kind of tell." He said as he stretched and reluctantly got out of bed, walking into the restroom and starting his morning ritual. Stacy looked around and found her clothes, but didn't really feel like putting them on, she felt a bit embarrassed and sat in the bed, waiting for James to finish whatever he was doing. She happened to glance over towards the restroom and saw him brushing his teeth and washing his face, all while naked, making her blush slightly, her prudishness back in full force. James picked up on this as he stuck his head out briefly. "You're absolutely adorable when you blush; you're going to get me addicted to it at this rate."

This made it even worse for Stacy, embarrassing her so much she hid her face in her hands. She heard the shower turn on and uncovered her face only to see James standing in the doorway, still naked and smiling. "My shower takes a while to heat up, also would you hand me a towel? They're in the closet. Ah, never mind let me get it myself." He said as he walked across the room and did so, putting it over his shoulders and then standing right in front of Stacy, whose head was back in her hands as he rubbed her shoulder. "This is actually the perfect time for me to talk to you about what I had planned for my turn in our next TR session." The redness crept further down her face, spreading to her neck.

"Now?" She asked through her hands. "Yes indeed. You see, I think your desires run a bit deeper than we've gone just yet. I think you have a very significant submissive streak within you and I want to explore that." She was silent, not knowing what to say as she clenched her thighs together, hoping he wouldn't notice the movement. Not only did he notice though, he growled aloud and moved his hand from her shoulder to her cheek, caressing it firmly "Yep, yes indeed. I saw that, it makes you wet doesn't it? Man, if the word alone did the trick then you're going to cum without me even touching you once we get the session under way." Stacy felt him moving her hands away from her face and tried to keep them from doing so, but felt his insistence increase and soon stopped fighting him, though her resistance was a token in the first place.

"The TR session will take place in two days' time, until then its business as usual, no talking about it or anything. I won't be able to wait until then if I don't have you in the meantime, look at what you do to me." He said to her, moving his hand under her chin and gently tilting it up, bringing her eyes level with his fully hard cock and making her squirm and bite her lip to stifle the moan that came from within her. James stared into her eyes as she blushed harder and harder, feeling the wetness grow within her until she thought she might faint.

He nodded at her slightly and moved forward by a fraction of an inch, his cock bobbing gently as it moved a bit closer to her lips. She parted her lips and licked them, looking into his eyes and seeing another imperceptible nod before she leaned forward and kissed the tip of him softly, less a kiss and more her brushing her lips against it while exhaling slightly, making him groan in pleasure as his cock twitched visibly, seeming almost hungry, if not angry at her teasing. He stepped back from her and took her hand, standing her up and then pulling her into a deep hug. "Shower with me." He said into her ear, telling her and not asking. She hid her face in his neck and nodded, shuddering in pleasure as he licked her ear and grabbed her ass possessively before leading her into the restroom, opening the curtain and helping her into the warm spray as she sighed and closed her eyes. They stood together under the cascading water for a while,

James holding her from behind and then turning her to face him, smiling while staring deeply into her eyes, which would have been downcast had his gaze been less commanding. He held her eyes as he lathered her entire body with his large hands, moaning as he paid attention to every inch of her, blushing yet again as he worked her breasts, her nipples soon hard again despite the gentle heat of the water. The entire shower took place in silence and seemed to Stacy to last for hours, though in reality it was barely fifteen minutes. After lathering her body and rinsing her, James had her do the same for him, making sure she paid attention to his cock, putting her hand onto it when she tried to skip it in embarrassment. After the shower ended, he helped her out and put the towel around her shoulders, leading her to the bed and drying her off, sitting her down and on the edge of the bed. After she was dried off, he took the towel and held it close to his face and inhaled deeply. "You smell wonderful Stacy."

"James!" Was all she could say, her hands quickly hiding her face once more as James deep chuckle made her smile despite her burning embarrassment. He sat down next to her, his arm sliding around her waist, lower than usual, his large hand resting just above her ass and squeezing idly as he sighed in contentment and happiness. Stacy soon let her hands fall to her sides, then she hugged James close, her head on his chest as she sighed for the same reasons he had. "Stacy my dear, I'm seeing more and more that you've got submissive tendencies and I can't wait to explore them, is that something you want? I promise we'll go at the speed you like and that you'll enjoy learning about yourself as I do the same. What do you think?"

Stacy nodded into his chest, feeling him squeeze her again, his smile coming through in his voice. "I'm very glad you've chosen to let me take you deeper into what makes you the wonderful lady you are Stacy, I won't disappoint you, you'll see. Having a submissive nature is one thing, but a fetish for submission is another. Some people have one or the other; in your case it appears to be both. Basically this means that you both naturally desire to submit to a certain type of person as well as receiving sexual enjoyment from it. Some people ignorantly imagine that this means that you submit to any and every one, but such couldn't be further from the truth. As you've shown me and told me, you have in the past manipulated others when you thought you would be able to do so successfully, so far from submitting to anyone you are quite selective about whom you do so with. Tell me Stacy, when was the first time you tried to control me? Do you remember? I certainly do." He said as he hugged her close.

"The first time was...in the car on the way to the coffee shop, when I asked you about...lust." She said, recalling the surge she had felt when he turned her teasing back onto her and the even greater one that lanced through her when he had first told her not to interrupt him. She moaned into him as his hands massaged her, not in the way they did for her relief, but purely to give her sexual pleasure as they reminisced.

"Mmm-hmm that was it. Back at the bar I went over three different ways to try to get your attention, I debated between the one I ended up doing, or buying you another round and just curling my finger at you and mouthing the words 'come here'. How would you have reacted if I'd done that babe?"

Stacy bit her lip while she re-imagined the fateful scene that night, trying to recall her mind state after the dancing groper, the try hard and the drunks.

"I can't really say now to be honest, I was fed up for sure with the same old scene, so that would have gotten you some points for being different, as well as some for being direct, I'd say it would have come down to a 50-50 split second type of thing." She mused, licking James' nipple quickly and feeling the shiver run through him.

"Mmm...I can tell that part of you likes being ordered around, but it seems like you fight yourself a bit, why is that?" He said as he sucked her earlobe. Stacy shrugged, still leaning into his chest, not really being able to pin down the reason. James kissed her, then grinned. "Let's try it out right now. Stand up." Stacy did so quickly, trying not to be reluctant about it, wanting to please him. "You don't have to jump to it like that babe, I'm not your drill sergeant...unless that turns you on I guess." Stacy laughed and shook her head; she had no fetish for being yelled at. Suddenly James stood up and snapped. "I got it, we'll do a photo shoot and pretend we're in a studio...well, we kind of are, this is a studio apartment, but you know what I mean. Imagine I've got a big camera pointed right at you. Alright Stacy, take a few steps back for me baby, a few more, good...now hold it, turn to the side, look back over your shoulder and smile for me." Stacy felt a bit silly at first, but when she saw how engrossed James was then she began to take it seriously too, listening to him intently and trying to hold the poses he asked for, strangely not feeling any embarrassment at all, despite being naked. James went to his dresser and pulled out a large polo shirt, then tossed it to her. "That's a relic from my heavier days, but I just realized that on you it would look incredibly hot. Put it on for me and let me take a few shots, just with my phone, nothing fancy." Stacy unfolded the shirt and held it up to herself; it went down to just above her pelvis. Suddenly she became shy again and James slid a bit further into his role as a photographer, goading her onward. "Come on Stacy, this will be too hot for words, think of all your adoring fans!" He said with a wink, holding his smart phone up and turning it sideways, heightening Stacy's embarrassment tenfold as the camera flash burned away all of her previous boldness. James stared at her with undisguised lust, his cock growing as he tried to keep taking pictures, but soon he was fully erect and put the camera down, tossing it onto the bed and rushing to her, pulling her into a deep kiss that surprised her due to its intensity. His hands grabber her rear end firmly and pulled her forward as his tongue pushed deep into her mouth, pressing down her own as he sucked her lips, making her eyelids flutter as her desire for a dominant kiss was fulfilled.

"Man...when you blush like that it is so hard for me not to just pounce on you right then and there. I don't know why I find it so hot, probably because of how quiet you get and the vulnerability you exude during those moments. At the same time though, part of me wants to stop making you feel that way and hug you, but you seem to enjoy situations where you get...hmm...taken advantage of. Is that correct my dear?"

Stacy hung her head and nodded, but James lifted her chin and kissed her softly.

"Baby, don't you dare feel ashamed of what you like, you can and will feel that way about a great many things, but I won't allow you to feel embarrassed about that. You are a beautiful and intelligent woman, what turns you on is a beautiful facet of your personality and I am honored to help you explore it. Apologies though, I interrupted you, continue. Why do you enjoy being taken advantage of? You can feel embarrassed now." He said as his eyes bored into her soul, not letting her avert her gaze as she spoke and making her feel even more exposed than she had in front of the camera.

"I...enjoy feeling helpless, like there's nothing I can do so I should just go along with the situation I've gotten myself into. It feels exhilarating and if the situation includes me being...you know..." She trailed off as James took over for her.

"Includes you being...pushed around? Commanded? Pressured into things you wouldn't do otherwise? I should have known, you didn't even want a safe word with our first session...I want to have one in the future though, since it seems you're okay with the heavier stuff, I would just feel better if we had one, and really it would make it possible for MORE of your limits to be pushed, it won't put a damper on things at all."

Stacy thought hard about it; still feeling like a safe word would ruin the scenario for her as the trepidation showed on her face.

"Let's just try it with one, just a quick replay of the last scene, except now I won't stop unless you say the safe word, instead of me breaking the scene when you get a little nervous, okay?" Stacy nodded happily, glad he didn't try to force her to agree. "I have some jeans you can wear with that shirt, put em on and then come back into this room once you're ready to start, and it will be on, no stopping until you use the safe word or we both cum. What do you want to use as the word? Make it something that won't possibly come up during the session." Stacy smiled, again thinking back to the night they met. "How about grasshopper?"

James laughed and nodded, getting the jeans out and tossing them to her. "That's perfect, here are the jeans, they won't make your ass look as awesome as the things you usually wear, but you won't keep them on for long once the scene starts. I don't know you and you're a college student answering an ad off the internet about making lots of money with no experience needed." He said with a wink.

"And you are a manipulative, overbearing photographer who

takes advantage of girl like me whenever you can." Stacy said as she smiled, feeling herself getting wet already as she pulled the jeans on and then walked out of the room. James followed her into the living room and rearranged the coffee table to look like a desk of sorts in front of his recliner. "Go out the front door real quick and then knock, it will mark the start of the scene." Stacy calmed her nerves and hoped she would at least think about using the safe word, then took a deep breath and walked back inside.

James sat in his chair and nodded curtly to her when she entered.

"You didn't knock, I like a girl whose forward. What brings you here to my office today? Are you needing a photoset done for something, a wedding or party perhaps?"

"No, I'm actually here about an ad I saw online"

"Which one? I have one asking for voluptuous women for hostess jobs and various ones for modeling. What are you looking to do?"

"Well, I need money for college so I want to model and make enough to pay for it."

"Ah, okay, tuition is a killer out there, to say nothing of books, I understand! Looking at you I can see that you have two of the asset I'm looking for in a model for a couple of specific shoots, let me get my camera ready here... all right then, stand up for me."

Stacy raised an eyebrow. "Is that it? There's nothing I have to fill out? Don't you want to see my I.D?"

"One thing you'll learn in this biz is that we move fast, plus I'm getting you on camera so it will be fine. If you make the cut and everything goes well then I'll get your information I need from you once we finish up. Now then, let's start off with some headshots, go ahead and stand up for me." James said, waving off her trepidation. She stood up and he began snapping off pictures, each shutter sound making her a bit more aroused as she wondered how far he would take things and tried to think of ways to push him as he played up his nice guy angle, encouraging her. "Okay, just be natural, be yourself and smile for me."

Snap

"Great, now turn to the side for me"

Click

"Good, good. Gimme that smile!"

Click

"Alright, now turn to the other side."

Click

"Aaaaaaaand there we go, all done with the headshots! Now then, let's go ahead and do some more upper body shots minus the shirt, take it off." Stacy was genuinely surprised by both the photographers forwardness and by her own reaction; she went beet red and began to fidget and stammer.

"Um...no..thank you...but no." The photographer sighed and rubbed his temples, seeming so genuinely irritated that Stacy felt a twinge of nervousness in her, but as she remembered the safe word and saw a slight wink then she regained her composure and her desire to push the lecherous man before her. She grew slightly more defiant and shook her head firmly, with conviction. "No, I don't even know your name, you're just trying to take advantage of me, I'm leaving!" She said as she walked toward the door. In a flash, the photographer was between her and the door, with a very different look on his face. Gone was the easygoing smile from before, replaced with a the same eager, yet stern and commanding expression a lot like the one Joe had at several points during her study session.

"I don't think you understand honey, you see, I'm ALREADY into this shoot, so if you're trying to stop before it's over then I'm out time AND money. That's not how I do things, so let's finish the shoot, okay?" As he spoke, he had moved ever so slightly into Stacy's personal space a centimeter at a time, causing her to slowly back away from him until she was back in the center of the room. He raised the camera again and clicked pictures off, but this time his manner was nothing like the jovial, encouraging one he had used before. Now he was certain he had the upper hand and simply told her what to do, no longer asking. The requests he made also grew more and more explicit and as she was forced to comply, her blushing grew by orders of magnitude, along with his arousal.

"Alright, since you wanted to be difficult before, we'll start slow. Undo the top button on that shirt."

Click

"Undo another one."

Click

Click

"Two more, let me and the camera see what you've been hiding in there all this time."

Click

"No bra? Maybe that's why you didn't want to take it off, didn't want to come across as a slut. I'll tell you what, undo all the buttons, but don't take the shirt off."

Stacy felt indignant at the photographers usage of the word slut in relation to her, even peripherally, but held it in, realizing that he had the power as it was and complying to keep things moving, her breathing heavy as she hoped that time would stop before she had to take off her pants, wet as she was there wasn't any way he wouldn't both see and comment on such, let alone taking advantage of her arousal. Nonetheless, she complied, taking her time with each button and feeling a bit of a power shift as she kept him waiting.

"Look honey, we're burning daylight here, hurry it up. Alright, good. Now just kind of let the shirt hang open, like you didn't mean for it to, you just forgot it was open and were walking around like that. No, you're not giving me the pose, think of the shirt. Here let me do it, just stand right there."

Stacy drew back when he moved toward her with his hand out, but she was quickly overcome as he held her arms, putting them down to her sides with a sigh as he grabbed both sides of the shirt and fluttered them, making it open all the way down and show a sliver of her smooth skin, starting from her neck and extending all the way down to just below her navel. The photographer stepped back, satisfied and snapped more pictures.

Click

Click

Click

Click

"Alright that's good, you're a bit stiff but that actually helped then, just stay still and let me pose you how I need to since you can't get the pose right on your own, understand?" Stacy rolled her eyes and scoffed. "I SAID do you understand? I don't like this attitude of yours, are we having a breakdown in communications? If you don't want to do this and feel like paying for the time and labor I've spent thus far and leaving then you go right ahead, but if you want to finish this shoot and not owe a dime then I want to hear a yes sir, and that's how you'll answer me for the duration of this shoot, understood?"

"Yes sir."

"That's what I like to hear, and I better not see you rolling your eyes again either. Now lose the shirt completely and be quick about it." He said, watching with undisguised glee as Stacy crossed her arms over her chest, then slowly lowered them and took the shirt off, handing it to him meekly, the past power shift having swung far back in his favor. He tossed the shirt onto the bed and then took the chair from his desk and rolled it to her.

"Now then, turn around, let's see what you're working with around back." Stacy did so quickly, turning around 360 degrees, not wanting to have him stare at her backside any longer than a second or so. When she turned back to face him, she knew he wouldn't accept that by his expression. "Okay, this isn't ballet class honey, I didn't ask you to pirouette, I said I wanted to see what you look like around BACK, so why am I looking at your front right now? 180 degrees please, get to turning, chop chop." This time Stacy felt his eyes on her rear intently and squirmed around in the silence, hearing him groan slightly. "Well, well, well, the jeans try to hide it, but they can't hide it all, not from me anyway. I'm going to need a better look at that, lose the pants, get them about around your knees." At this point Stacy hesitated again, hoping he wouldn't press her, wishing she wasn't so aroused but feeling the hope evaporate and the wish disappear unfulfilled as he grabbed the hem of the jeans and tugged them down, scoffing as he did and making her jump. "Wow, all that stuff about being nervous and whatever when we started this photo-shoot and here you aren't even wearing underwear. You'd better be glad you've got a wondrous looking ass here. Man that is nice. Stay right there, don't move a muscle, I'm going to get some good shots of it."

Click

Click

Click

Click

Click

"Great, these are gold. Now you get to use that chair, put on knee up on it and look over your shoulder at me. No, arch your back more, trust me, I know what guys want to see. Yeah, a little more...No. You're giving me that nervous garbage again? Like I said, if you can't give me the poses I want then I'm going to have to do it myself. Stay there." She felt his breath heavy on her neck as his body pressed against hers from the back, far closer than the photo-shoot required. His hands roamed up and down her body, rubbing her sides, grabbing her cheeks lewdly and running upwards to cup her breasts. "I think I can definitely get you into the scene with assets like you've got, but the final question is this: are you willing to...do what it takes to get started in this business? If I'm your agent then I'm the one you're going to want to keep happy, that way I will be able to keep you happy, understand?" As she nodded and turned her head to kiss him, she recalled that he wasn't James, but the photographer and stopped short. The photographer looked concerned for a moment but continued groping her as he asked her what was the matter. "I have a boyfriend; I can't do this with you!"

The photographer pinched her nipples sharply, making her gasp as he rolled them in his hands and tugged them forward, making them hard to the touch. She felt herself surrendering to the sensations as the hands used on her were those of James, teasing, heavy and knowledgeable as to all of her erogenous zones despite the face and voice being that of the photographer.

"Just don't tell him, this is work and that's your personal life. We're not even doing anything right now, I'm just getting you ready for your shoot, that's all. I need your nipples hard so that's why I'm pinching them. I'm sure he would understand this is just something that happens in a photo-shoot, like kissing scenes in a movie. Now then, there's just one more thing I need from you today and you'll be in, a full blown model and ready to sign all the release papers and then we can get you out to some shoots, start paying off those pointlessly expensive books they force you to buy in college, what a racket eh?" Stacy nodded, smiling at the photographers disarming charm when she should have been wary of it, as it only came in the beginning and before something he expected her to say no to.

"Go ahead and sit in the chair and I'll explain the last thing to you."

Stacy sat in the chair and immediately noticed that he wasn't moving out of her personal space, meaning her face was now level with his crotch, which still bulged forward, tenting his slacks lewdly. When she tried to roll the chair backwards and away from him, he put his hand on the arm of the chair and shook his head silently, switching to his gaze that pulled her eyes into it, making her stare at him as he rubbed her shoulder, then moved downward, brushing over her nipples as if he was no longer interested in them since he had already had them. He grabbed her slender hand and placed it onto the tented area of his pants, nodding as he did so. Stacy shook her head.

"I have a boyfriend...I can't." The photographer switched to his disarming smile yet again, circling around her wounded resolve like a wolf around a limping deer. "Get your mind out of the gutter honey, I don't want anything but a handshake...the thing is, since you're going to be making my cock hard a lot during these shoots, you may as well get used to it, so you're just going to get to know it a bit, meet him and greet him. All I want is your pretty little hand, it's the same as a handshake you'll just be taking a different, more important part of me in your hand." At this he unzipped and as she continued to stare into the abyss in his slacks until she saw his cock slowly extend and engorged, going from flaccid to full length in 30 seconds of silence that made her consider the safe word due to how nervous she felt and how insistent both the photographer as well as his cock were being. She almost felt the will of his dick, twitching and straining in an obscene manner as it anticipated her touch, preparing its venom for release once it was finished with her. The photographer snapped pictures still, no longer encouraging her but feeding off of her trepidation and embarrassment, each shutter sound moving her closer and closer to the point of no return as her subconscious mind screamed at her that it was just a game and that James wouldn't be mad at her. He saw her move her hand slightly and settled down, knowing he had won. It was now just a waiting game. Stacy timidly put her hand out, then grabbed the photographers cock, feeling it jerk as he chuckled derisively, sure of his victory.

"Yeah, good girl. You've already come this far, time to seal the deal. Jerk it harder, take a nice firm grip, there you go. Good, the deal is getting close to being sealed, these pictures are the hottest I've ever taken...look at it straight, drop the scared act, you know you like it, your nipples are still hard."

The constant mind games the photographer was playing with her as well as her nervousness threatened to overcome her at any moment, even bringing her to the point of tears once, though she couldn't identify exactly why. Soon she was looking down and jerking him as fast as she could, genuinely wanting James to be back and for this crude, uncouth and overbearing photographer to disappear into the ether from which he appeared. She could tell he was close, his cock twitched and jerked even more sharply and frequently than before and he had ceased his snide remarks as her blushing deepened fully, and soon she felt the tightening that came before his climax. As she felt it she did her best to point his cock away from her but he grabbed it, overpowering her and pointing it at her face, hitting her squarely with all six long, hot ropes of sticky semen as he groaned loudly and fell back onto the bed. Stacy got up, feeling relieved as she grabbed a tissue from the dispenser near his nightstand and tried to wipe her face before being stopped by the grinning photographer once more.

"Not just yet, you have to give me a picture of you wearing it!"

"Grasshopper!" Stacy yelled as she hopped back, nearly

tripping as James returned and held his arms open to her while smiling. She fell into them and felt all her negative feelings wash away as he hugged them out, pouring his own care and tenderness into her to replace them.

"So what do you think? Safe words make it more intense eh?" She smiled and nodded as she kissed him.

"I wanted to say it so many times..."

"I could tell! I wanted to myself a few times, but I kept pushing myself, I wasn't trying to make you say it, I just wanted you to WANT to say it, if that makes sense." Stacy nodded again, and then got an idea.

"I bet you can't even remember what the next scene is supposed to be" She said, hoping his post orgasm bliss would make his lips loose.

"You get interviewed for a new job in the customer service department of a sex toy company...Hey, I said no asking about it!" She smiled and turned over, letting him spoon her as she giggled and drifted off to sleep, feeling her excitement increase at what the next time would bring.

BOOK 4: JOB OPPORTUNITY

After tricking James into revealing the plot of their next total role play session, Stacy had spent the rest of the morning and with him, most of that time in his arms. Once late morning came they reluctantly parted, Stacy to go home and change before going to work, James to begin preparing for the session that would take place in two days' time. She had tried several more times to get him to tell her more about how things would take place and almost got angry at him when he said that he planned to involve more people this time, her eyes widening as she stood up indignantly. Her momentary anger was quickly washed away when his voice became stern and he told her to sit back down and not to interrupt.

"I don't mean what you seem to think I meant by involving more people this time Stacy my dear. All I mean is that there will be some other people who are in on the session as secondary characters to add even more realism to the atmosphere, understand?" Stacy went red yet again and apologized for jumping once more to a conclusion, something she had been making a conscious effort to do less. After revealing that he refused to say any more no matter how much she goaded and coaxed him. On her way home her mind was abuzz with thoughts as she wondered who he had in mind, what they would be doing and if she knew them or not, feeling herself begin to get excited at the many unknowns that loomed in front of her. She trusted James implicitly and had no apprehension about any of it, just barely contained enthusiasm and joy that almost made her giddy with anticipation. She thought of calling Cheryl, but decided to just talk to her at work. As she showered she couldn't help wishing James was there with her, imagining his strong arms encircling her and his hot breath on her neck. Without him there, the shower became a monotonous drudge and was over within 8 minutes.

Afterwards she got dressed in her standard work attire, a knee length pencil skirt, white blouse and her favorite low heels. She stood in front of her mirror and turned, looking herself over and smiling as she imagined James complimenting her either verbally or his favored way: grabbing some part of her and pulling her to him and then complimenting her. she blushed and walked away from the mirror as she recalled how much time he had spent massaging her rear end, amazed that he enjoyed it so much as it had made her the target of much teasing ever since middle school.

"You have to know that they were jealous and nothing more, there's just no way it was anything else babe. Having hips and an ass like yours would only be a bad thing for a man who wasn't much of a man and had no idea what to do to take care of a girl endowed as you are. I could grab and squeeze on your ass all day every day for the next 20 years and be happy as a clam." Reveling in the words she replayed again and again in her mind she nearly missed the exit to her job, shaking her head as she got off the highway and pulled into the parking garage. As she walked up to the door of the massive call center, she grew weary, something she hadn't ever felt before. She had never minded the job in the past as she did it solely to keep busy but now her mind was alight with expectations about her next session as well as thoughts of James himself. She went to the area she usually sat in and found an empty cubicle, logging in and starting her time automatically, thinking about any and everything but her job. Next to her on the left was Tiffani, a kind and sweet woman who always helped her out when she needed a break or got an annoying customer and on the right was Cheryl, who hadn't noticed her yet as she was on a call. Stacy decided to wait until Cheryl finished and then talk to her, keeping her pc on break mode and not logging in to take calls so she wouldn't be pulled away. She felt less than angry at her, more confused than anything else due to the remarks she had made the last time they spoke over the phone, after the first night she had met James and had been flustered. When Cheryl finished her call, ending with a polite 'thank you for calling and have a nice day', she rolled her eyes with exasperation and slid her chair away from her cubicle, noticing Stacy as she did. "Hey Cheryl, are you feeling better today?" Stacy asked, surprised at herself since she was typically very non-confrontational. Cheryl raised one eyebrow.

"What are you talking about Stacy? I haven't been sick." She said.

"Not sick, you seemed upset or something the last time I called you, it was almost a week ago, but I called you after I met someone and asked-" Cheryl nodded as she recalled the conversation. "Oh right, I wasn't upset, it just felt like you were calling to gloat over how happy you were." Stacy scoffed and tried to keep her tone polite but inside she was feeling quite angry, wanting to tell Cheryl that her constant negative attitude was really annoying. Despite this she held her tongue and softened, having nothing to gain from being insulting to her in return.

"Cheryl, we've been friends since I started here and we've both talked about our relationships, what do you mean gloating? I was nervous and wanted to talk to someone about it so I called you, and you asked if anything else happened! What good would it do me to be insulting toward you?"

Before Cheryl could answer the floor supervisor walked down their aisle in a flurry, stopping near them.

"Ladies, I cannot have two of my agents in break mode when they aren't on scheduled breaks, we have FIVE calls in queue! That's nearly 8, which is the cutoff point! I expect better of the two of you, you're usually good at staying on task! Come on folks, five in queue, that's yellow alert! Let's kick the queue down, remember: we are quality! Say it with me now, on three!"

Stacy and Cheryl went back to their cubicles and mirthlessly echoed the chant, then got back to taking calls, both of them feeling upset for different reasons as the day wore on.

After taking an interminable number of mundane calls, all either about setting up appointments for technicians to come to residences or customer service issues with various electric products, Stacy could deal with it no more and took her first fifteen minute break, logging out of call mode on her pc, putting her headset away and walking to the break room. Once she sat down she tried to think of some reason for her to be there, first in the break room and then at the call center at all, but none came to her mind, all she kept thinking of was how much she enjoyed being with James, how badly she wanted to call him or even better, just go over to his place or have him come to hers. She noticed Tiffani sitting at the table opposite to hers and smiled at her, which made Tiffani give her a knowing grin.

"So, what's his name Stacy?" She asked as Stacy looked down sheepishly.

"Is it that obvious?" She asked, getting a chuckle and a nod in return. She got up and sat with Tiffani, then told her everything. Tiffani listened patiently as she explained how they had met but shied away from the details of their lovemaking, only saying that he had been very passionate and enjoyed role playing with her which made her blush. She also mentioned how strange Cheryl had been acting, both when she had called and this morning. In response Tiffani nodded sadly.

"Stacy, I hate to say it but when you're as happy and fulfilled as you obviously are, there are only two sorts of people: Those that are happy for and those that wish they were you. It's the same for your boyfriend and any men he knows as well; it's just how people are unfortunately."

Stacy didn't think that could be the case, but it did explain

Cheryl's abrupt and sarcastic comments, which made her feel upset, but more disappointed.

"Isn't Cheryl married though? I don't have anything for her to be jealous about! "Tiffani shrugged.

"Some people aren't able to have all their needs met with a relationship for whatever reason, it's not only about sex, there are emotional and mental aspects as well as the need for communication and companionship of a non-sexual kind. If any one of those areas is lacking, it can lead to negative emotions developing. I can't speak for Cheryl, but just try not to be too upset at her. I'm really happy for you myself; you have been glowing ever since you came in today."

Stacy smiled and thanked Tiffani for her advice, then got up and headed out of the break room to spend her last three hours taking calls before her shift ended.

Three hours later Stacy stood up and stretched, grateful that her shift had finally ended and she could leave. The last three hours of her shift had been even more boring than the first two and she resisted the urge to run from the place or quit on her way out. As soon as she got to her car she called James, smiling at how he answered within one or two rings whenever she called.

"Hey babe, how's it going? How was work?"

"Fine, boring but fine, my friend Cheryl is still being rude though. What are you doing right now?"

"Planning and plotting for a hot date, it's a secret though, very hush-hush, I can't say a word about it I'm afraid."

"Do you have time to eat something or is your plotting filling your schedule?" She asked with a grin.

"I always have time for you, do you want to go somewhere, or come over here or what? Do you know how to cook?"

"I'm okay, nothing too fancy though, how about you?"

"I know my way around the kitchen, if I didn't I'd have starved or never escaped my 'funny fat guy' stage. Why don't you come over and I'll make something? It will work better that way because I can put part one of my plan into action as well."

Stacy agreed and was soon on her way to his apartment, giddy with excitement about whatever part of his plan was going to be put into action, the events of her workday fading slowly into the back of her mind. When she arrived and entered, she was greeted by wonderful smells, garlic, onions and olive oil being the ones she placed the quickest. She entered the kitchen and saw James sliding two chicken breasts onto as many pieces of bread, then pouring the fragrant mixture of olive oil she had smelled before onto them before putting them into the oven. After he finished he washed and dried his hands and then held his arms out to her, giving her a huge hug, her favorite type. She pressed herself into his chest and giggled as his hands gave her rear end several squeezes, something she was quickly becoming used to.

"What was that you were working on before you started groping me?" She asked as she kissed his chin quickly.

"That is Bruschetta, something I've been trying to perfect for a while now. I think it should come out well this time, it will be finished in five minutes, which is exactly how long I plan to grope you for, so it's a win for everyone involved!" He said as he pulled her onto the couch, sitting her in his lap, her legs across both of his knees as they kissed deeply while one of his hands rubbed up her sides underneath her shirt and the other stayed firmly on her backside.

She soon felt his hardness pressing into her thighs and shifted slightly, moving her hand from his neck down to grab at the bulge in his shorts, eliciting a groan from him as he sucked her neck and worked his hand under her bra, squeezing her left breast and teasing the nipple until it stood at attention, shivers of pleasure running through her body. She shifted position, straddling him and slowly grinding on his lap as he felt her and licked up the side of her neck, nipping her ear and making her shudder and lean into him, wishing the Bruschetta would finish so they could dispense with the foreplay. She moved her free hand around to grab his hand that had been feeling her rear end and placed it at the hem of her jeans, feeling him harden further as he slipped it into them and felt her ass again, covered now by only her panties. He lifted her shirt and pulled down her bra on the right side and began working on that breast, the nipple hardening as he formed a seal around it with his lips and licked it until it was engorged, soon switching to the left and giving it the same treatment. She held his head in her hands and pressed it into her chest, feeling him lick and lightly nip down the valley between her breasts, finding a hitherto unknown erogenous zone for her: the center of her chest, just above her sternum. She shuddered and arched her back involuntarily as he made contact with the area, making a mental note to pay it more attention later as Stacy closed her eyes and held him closer still, forgetting about everything but the electric pleasure surging through her body. Soon she noticed him waving his hands instead of feeling them on her and she blushed when she let his head go and he leant back and gasped several times.

"Whew, you took a fellows breath away there babe, quite literally! For one, I think the Bruschetta is about finished and for two, I've got to catch my breath, you just sit tight and I'll be right back. Aw come on, don't be embarrassed, I think it's flattering to make you so aroused you try to smother me." He said as she hid her face in her hands. He took the Bruschetta out of the oven and put it onto two plates, and then set both down at the small coffee table; it smelled even better than it had at first! He then went back into the kitchen and soon called out to her, asking if she cared for any wine. She agreed and soon he came back with two long stem glasses and a bottle of red wine in a small pail of ice. He poured them both a glass and then they began eating. The Bruschetta turned out beautifully, the chicken was tender and juicy, the sour dough was crisp on the outside and fluffy on the inside and the sauce tasted wonderful, highlighting the tastes and bringing them out. None of the tastes was overpowering and the wine went perfectly with the meal. After they finished James looked expectantly at Stacy.

"So, what do you think? Did you enjoy it?"

"Absolutely James, it was delicious! I've never had Bruschetta before but I hope to have that again sometime!" She said enthusiastically. He smiled and thanked her for the compliment, looking relieved. Stacy offered to do kitchen clean up but he refused adamantly.

"Nope, that's not what you're here for babe, you had a long day at work and I told you before to just sit right there, let me handle this stuff. In fact, tell me about your day, how did it go?" He said as he got up and put the dishes into the sink, leaving the wine on the table. When he came back, Stacy had refilled both their glasses, hers a bit higher than his.

"So your day was that bad huh?" James said as he sat near her, putting his arm around her.

Stacy went on to tell him about Cheryl and her continued rudeness, how she accused her of gloating about meeting him and then about speaking with Tiffani and the good advice she gave. James took one drink of his wine as he listened intently to her and once she finished recapping her day and telling him that she was thinking of quitting she took another drink of her wine, draining half of it and sighing, feeling its warmth spreading through her along with relief and the pleasure of his arm around her.

"That doesn't sound like a fun at all babe, I'm sorry you had to deal with all of that negativity, some people quite literally can't stand to see anyone else happy, even if they're relatively fulfilled and even less if they aren't, which sounds like the case with this Cheryl. If you want to quit then you should, you are blessed with not having a whole lot of stress in your life and there's no reason for you to take on more if it doesn't do anyone any good, and I've actually had an idea after hearing that, I think a slight change to our upcoming role-play session is in order, but don't worry, it will be for the positive, depending on your performance. I was going to put part one of the session into action now, but first I think you could do with a bit of stress release."

Stacy was feeling the alcohol begin to affect her and said that she wanted to see what the change was, but James kissed her swiftly and then stood up, his voice growing stern and commanding, making her blush and grow wet instantly.

"No. That comes later. Stretch out on the couch, on your stomach."

She quickly complied without a word, glad to have her reddened face hidden from his view and began to moan as his hands ran lightly over her body, touching her shoulders, running down her sides, stroking her back, moving down the cleft of her ass to her thighs and descending to her calves, then stopping, nearly making her whimper at how quickly it was over.

"Stand up for me Stacy, let me undress you." James told her simply. She did so, her arms crossed in front of her until he took them and raised them, sliding her shirt up and off in a smooth motion, leaving her wishing he would remove her bra, though he didn't. He then moved in front of her and unzipped her jeans while staring into her eyes, making her unable to look away no matter how much she wanted to as the jeans slid slowly into a pool at her feet and he led her out of them and had her stretch back out on the couch as she had before, feeling ten times more exposed and so aroused she was glad her panties had stayed on. His hands no longer worked lightly and quickly, their action was firm and soothing, but insistent as he attacked the stress that had built up in her through her day, melting it with a combination of the heat from his hands and that from her arousal. She soon moaned aloud, feeling herself grow more relieved as her muscles loosened up, both shoulders doing so at the same time. She felt him lighten his touch and spend a few more moments on her shoulders, moving down her shoulder blades and increasing the pressure once again on the small of her back. She felt a slight discomfort and groaned lightly, but it went away quickly as her back loosened up and she moaned appreciatively. She wondered what he would do next, whether he would skip her rear end and come back to it like he had the first time or if he wouldn't be able to resist touching her there, and she felt him hesitating, smiling and wiggling her hips ever so slightly, making him lose the fight he was having with himself and grab her ass firmly, squeezing and rubbing it as she grew wet and clenched her legs together.

When he noticed that, he moved down to her thighs and spread them, whispering sternly to her that she was to remain loose. She nodded and let him pry her thighs apart, the redness creeping down her neck and to her shoulders as he noticed how wet she was.

"My, I think I know a faster way to relieve the last of your stress. Sit up and spread your legs." He said, helping her into position and pulling her panties halfway off with his teeth as she squirmed and felt hot with arousal and embarrassment. The embarrassment began to lose ground when his face disappeared between her legs and he began planting teasing kisses and light bites all over her inner thighs as his hands pulled her into him from behind. She gasped at the quickness with which he worked and soon had her hands back in his thick, curly hair and was trying to resist squeezing her legs together as she bit her lip and stifled a loud moan. She felt as if she could cum at any moment and he hadn't even gotten inside of her yet, and when he stopped and breathlessly told her to spread her lips for him, she did so quickly, eager to feel his tongue within her. Instead of diving in like she hoped he would however, he resumed teasing her, licking and sucking her fingers and blowing lightly onto them, then into her, making her dizzy with need as she tried to push his head further in, then tried to push herself against him. He resisted and she received a light swat on her backside, making her calm down and hold still. he tortured her for another two minutes that felt like hours, then licked into her and kissed her clitoris as he slid his finger into her, sending her over the edge and into her first orgasm as she gasped out loud and clenched around his finger, barely keeping from screaming as his tongue worked at her swelling clit through the waves of pleasure that emanated from within her and made her mind briefly go blank. When she regained her composure he was rubbing his neck and tasting the finger that had just been inside of her with a grin.

"You taste even better than the wine," He said as she rushed forward and kissed him deeply, tasting herself on his lips as she wrapped her arms around him, all the stress of the day becoming little more than a distant memory. They lay together on the couch for a few minutes, Stacy recovering her energy and basking in the glow that came from such relief as long as she could.

Soon James stood up and stretched, then sat back down and faced her. "Stacy, I want you to help me with my work. As you know I work for myself and have several businesses with a few clients each, in various fields. Instead of pretending to do customer service, why don't you try working with me?"

Stacy was very surprised by the supposed 'little change' and didn't know what to say at first, but as she thought about how much they enjoyed their time together and how stressful her current job had become, she nodded. James smiled and kissed her, then gave her a small card with a website on it.

"This is the website for the consulting company I freelance for, go here after you get home and you'll see a link to the application. If it's accepted then you'll have an interview and be on your way." He said with a wink. Stacy pocketed the card and then kissed him again, thanking him for spending so much time and effort planning things for them to do.

"Hey, nothings too much work for you babe, besides, this is the most fun I can ever remember having! It's not even about the sex, though that is amazing, I enjoy spending time with you and giving both of our minds a chance to flex their creative muscles and it goes both ways. If you've ever got any scenes or ideas you'd like to try, or even something you'd like me to do, then I want you to ask, no matter what, understand?" He said as she nodded in his embrace. She wanted to spend the rest of the evening with him, but his computer began making a ringing noise and he apologized, then rushed to grab it, bringing the laptop back and sitting down right alongside her again as he opened it. She looked away from the screen at first, but he smiled and told her he had nothing to hide and she took a quick glance to see what had pulled him away from her, feeling a minor twinge of jealousy.

At first she couldn't tell what he was doing because of how fast he switched between windows, but he explained that he was chatting with a client as well as looking for more work.

At this Stacy asked what types of work he did, since she had never understood freelancing as a whole. James told her that he did writing, tech support and web design among other things.

"So I don't bore you, I basically do anything and everything I think I can do well enough to be paid for it. I've done some strange requests, like installing monitoring software on a pc to catch an unfaithful spouse and writing a very specific erotic story for someone with a very unique fetish. It's fun and challenging, I couldn't survive in the nine to five rat race. I'd rather be challenged and take the possible stress that comes with it than constantly be struggling to keep from falling asleep.

I'm sorry babe, but this client has me and I don't get to talk to them often, they'll probably want to...yep, they want to talk over the phone. I'll make it up to you next time; this was supposed to be about you."

Stacy kissed him, telling him that she felt wonderful and that as far as she was concerned, it HAD been all about her. They reluctantly got up and he walked her to her car, hugging her close the whole time. They kissed again before she got inside and soon she was on her way back home, refreshed and eager to hear from him again.

Later that evening after taking a nap, Stacy felt like talking to someone about James' offer for her to work with him, but could think of nobody that she could do so with. She decided instead to go to the website James had mentioned and sat at her computer, taking the card out of her purse and entering the address. She saw a professional looking site and after looking around a bit, a link for employment opportunities. The page it linked to had several more links on it, one for a chat, one for more information and one for the application itself, which she clicked quickly, feeling her heart rate increase as she did so. The application loaded up and her eyes grew wide at it, blushing as she saw some quite non-standard questions. Bust size, hip width, several check boxes for fetishes and even a section asking her to list two erogenous zones! She thought about calling James, but noticed a second phone number at the bottom of the application as well as a link to the chat if there were any questions. She wondered if she would be speaking to James if she used the chat, then decided to try it, clicking the link and watching the chat window load up, the small red 'Offline' light making her heart sink. After a minute though, it turned green and a message appeared.

"Thank you for your interest, you are now speaking to one of our human resource experts!"

She waited another few moments and soon a second message appeared.

"Hello, this is J; I see you came here from the application, how can I help you?"

She wondered if it was James, part of her felt it had to be, as he was the only one who would be online at a time like this, far past business hours for any company.

She typed: "Yes, I had some questions about the application."

"I understand. What would you like to know?"

"Some of the questions are...rather intimate."

"That isn't a question; it's a statement, though it is true. Are you aware of the position you are applying for?"

"Yes, but perhaps a bit more clarification would be helpful to me? I want to apply, but these questions are making me a bit nervous."

"I understand Stacy. Please ask any questions you have, I will do my best to help."

She smiled wide and then began typing.

"How do you know my name?!" Stacy asked, wanting to make James sweat a bit if she could.

At this there was a longer pause than normal on the chat window and soon her name in the previous message was replaced with the phrase 'prospective employee', making her smile as she knew she could only be speaking to James.

"I don't know what you mean, prospective employee."

"Never mind. I suppose the first question is about the bust size and hip width section."

"Ah, I understand. There is a strict dress code here at JM Consulting so we make certain that that is known from the start. Knowing our employee's measurements make certain aspects of human resources and accounting much easier, especially should disciplinary measures need to be taken to ensure adherence to the dress code."

Stacy felt a wave of arousal at the word 'disciplinary', ever since her first session with 'Joe'; she had become interested in it more and more.

"I have an idea, prospective employee. I will fill in the application for you; all you need to do is answer my questions."

Stacy was surprised, so much so that she would have refused if she wasn't certain she was talking to James. She answered the basic questions easily enough, but once the bust size question flashed across the screen, she felt nervous again and couldn't bring herself to answer. Soon another message appeared.

"I need to know your bust size Stacy, please answer this question. It is conditional for employment."

With her face burning red despite being alone, she typed her answer.

"34b"

"Good. Now your hip width. This too is conditional."

"I'm...not sure."

"Then stand up and check. I need this information to process your application."

After an extended pause during which Stacy pondered lying, she relented and checked, then sat back down.

"My jeans are size 32."

"For the duration of this interview, you are to address me as sir, is that clear?"

Stacy imagined James' eyes staring into her soul as his stern voice spoke the words of the message and grew even more aroused than she had been.

"Yes sir."

"Now then, one of your duties will be aiding in research for erotic stories, do you understand what this entails?"

"I believe so sir."

"I'll clarify it for you a bit: usually over chat, but sometimes over the phone, you will be expected to engage in various sexual situations, often referred to as cyber-sex and/or phone sex to add realism to the dialogue in the stories produced here. Realism and accuracy are important, so it will be your duty to be fully engaged during these research sessions, even if it becomes difficult to keep focused due to the nature of the research, understood?"

"Yes sir, I will do my best."

"We will see. Have you ever engaged in cyber-sex before?"

"No sir."

"That could be a problem Stacy, I am afraid we are looking for people with experience. If you would like, we can conduct a brief research session right now to ascertain whether or not you would be a good fit for this position."

"Is there any other way sir?"

"I'm afraid not."

"I understand. I will do it sir, please tell me what to do."

"That is a good attitude, we will begin simply. What are you wearing right now?"

"A t-shirt and jeans."

"All clothing descriptions are to include undergarments as well."

"Sorry sir, a t-shirt with no bra and jeans with panties underneath."

"What type of panties? Remember this will be used to add realism to stories, I expect detail."

"Yes sir. I am wearing a pair of bikini panties; they are black with lace around the edges."

"Good. Take off your jeans now."

Stacy complied with her demanding interviewer, feeling

somehow more aroused than if she had been standing in front of James as he acted like a different person. She did as he asked and then sat back down, conscious of the growing wetness in her panties as she typed.

"Yes sir."

"Are your nipples hard Stacy?"

Stacy blushed as her already hard nipples grew even harder at being mentioned.

"Answer my question Stacy."

"Yes sir."

And you haven't touched them, have you?"

"No sir."

"Good, it appears being given orders arouses you, which is quite useful for the position you applied for. You also seem to learn quickly and be a fast typist, all that's left now is the final part of the interview, the phone portion. We happen to have availability now; would you like to finish the process tonight?"

Stacy agreed, expecting to see James' number show up on her phone. To her surprise it was a totally different number despite the time, which threw her for a loop and almost made her not answer. Despite her trepidation however, she did.

"Hello?"

A gruff voice answered, one that didn't sound at all like James.

"Yes, Stacy? I'm calling from JM Consulting to finish the final part of your interview."

"Yes, thank you for accepting my application."

"The pleasure is all mine. You won't be meeting me in person as you'll be working with our freelancer out there, I believe you already know James correct?"

Stacy blushed and agreed, glad whoever was on the other line couldn't see her face.

"Good, you'll be acting as his assistant and research partner, I can see from the transcript here of your chat that you've got a can do attitude and a willingness to learn, among other assets that we here at JM Consulting find very attractive. One thing though, we don't allow inter-office relationships, it's a conflict of interest. Your relationship with James is to remain business or friendly and nothing more, anything else will be potentially subject to disciplinary action, is that understood?"

Stacy bit her lip as she lied for the first time in a long time.

"Yes, that's absolutely fine sir."

"Good, then you can consider yourself hired! Further details will be sent to the email address you provided in your chat, thank you for your time and we look forward to working with you."

After ending the call Stacy texted James to tell him she had been hired, then got an email from JM Consulting as James called her.

"Hey babe, I knew you would get it, you're awesome!"

"Thank you, though I can't help but feel like you put in a good word or two for me." She said with a smile.

"Who knows, all that matters now is that you get to work

with me instead of at that horrid office! You know Stacy...I can be a different person when it comes to work, I hope you understand that."

Feeling her arousal grow again, she asked what he meant.

"Well, I don't stop until the job is done, I can be demanding sometimes and if things require extra hours, I stay and make sure that everything gets taken care of. Can you handle that?"

"Yes James, I certainly can."

"Good. Additionally, being my assistant "He said, emphasizing the first three letters of assistant "may require you to...assume new positions on the fly, sometimes with little prior warning. Is that something you're comfortable with?"

"Yes James, of course." She said, feeling her nipples grow hard again.

"Great, this is going to be amazing. I want you to be here at 10:00 on the dot tomorrow, I have a story series about a girl like you who gets tired of the same old thing, I want to brainstorm some possible names and do a lot of research as far as the dialogue and content is concerned. If you come early then we can do some preliminary stress relief to get ready for the day" He said, his smile showing through in his voice.

"I can't wait James; I'll see you tomorrow morning!" Stacy said as she imagined what things the stress relief might entail. She went to bed excited and quite aroused, but certain that James would take care of it in the morning, smiling to herself as she drifted off, feeling a small surge of butterflies in her stomach at the new chapter of her life that was beginning.

www.ingramcontent.com/pod-product-compliance
Lightning Source LLC
LaVergne TN
LVHW081543060526
838200LV00048B/2193